Destined to Love

By Brenda Kennedy

Destined to Love

LULU EDITION

LULU ISBN: 978-1-312-52713-3

Dedicated to my children and grandchildren. I love you.

I would also like to dedicate this series to everyone who has survived domestic violence and to those who didn't.

Table of Contents

CHAPTER ONE: WILL YOU MARRY ME?

Angel

"I was scared, I thought you were giving me an engagement ring there for a minute," I say, looking at Mason. His eyes are dark, and he is rubbing his finger over his top lip. He is looking at me, but I don't think he sees me.

"I'm glad you like it, but I have something to ask you."

"Oh." Now my heart starts to beat a little faster and my palms sweat. "You do?"

His eyes are dark, and I can't read them.

Mason reaches in his jacket pocket, and pulls out a smaller black velvet box. He stands up, unbuttons his jacket, and kneels down on one knee in front of me. He looks so calm. He opens the velvet box and reveals a princess-cut engagement ring with a two-carat diamond set in gold.

"Angel," he says as he removes the engagement ring and lays the empty box on the table. He takes my left hand in his and strokes my knuckles with his thumb gently. "I have waited my whole life for you. When I first saw you, I knew I wanted you. I know we haven't known each other long, but we have been through so much already, and I know, without a doubt, that I want to spend every day of my life with you." Mason looks at me and smiles. "There is nothing that we can't handle together. I want you to be my wife, to be the mother of my children. I want us to grow old together. You are so beautiful and I love you." He smiles and holds the ring to my finger. "Angelica Hope Ramos Perez, will you marry me?"

I look at him with tears streaming down my eyes. "Mason?" I swallow the lump in my throat before I try to speak. "I love you, but there is something I have to tell you first."

"Oh, that's not the answer I was expecting."

"Here, sit down first." I stand up and pull his chair out for him to sit.

Mason stands, then sits down directly across from me, giving me his undivided attention. "It must be serious," he says, while leaning forward and resting his elbows on his knees. He clasps his hands together; I think it's to keep himself from fidgeting with the ring he is still holding.

"First of all, thank you for tonight. Dinner, the beautiful flowers, and my stunning past, present, and future necklace." I smile, and gently touch the necklace.

Mason just watches me and listens.

"I want you to know that I am so in love with you and I thank God, every day, for bringing you into my life." I wipe a few stray tears away using the back of my hand.

Mason leans over the table and takes my hand in his. "Beauty, whatever it is, just say it. There isn't anything that we can't work through. Whatever it is, I am here for you," he says while gently stroking my knuckles.

It's a sweet gesture that usually calms me instantly. I look up at Mason through wet eyelashes and blurred vision from crying. I clear my throat and say, "There's no easy way for me to say this and I regret having to tell you…"

"Beauty, please, it can't be…"

"I'm pregnant."

Mason just looks at me. Expressionless. He leans back in his chair before leaning forward again. My stomach does flip flops waiting for him to say something. He didn't stand up and walk out, so that's a good thing.

The maître'd walks past and Mason orders a double Scotch, before turning his attention back to me to ask, "Do you want anything?"

"No, I'm fine."

The maitre'd walks off. "How do you know?"

"I took a pregnancy test yesterday."

"You took one?" he asks, leaning back into his seat again. He places the beautiful princess-cut engagement ring on the table beside the black velvet box it came in.

"Three. I took three yesterday, I wanted to be sure."

The maitre'd shows up with Mason's double Scotch and Mason quickly orders another double. He downs his drink and hands the empty glass back to the maitre'd.

"Are you all right?" I ask, because I have never seen Mason drink like this before.

"It's a bit of a shock, that's all. I didn't consider this being a possibility. So, you took three pregnancy tests yesterday?" he asks, once the maitre'd is far enough away not to hear us. He leans forward in his seat again and runs his hands through his hair. I already know this is a sign of stress for Mason.

"I did. I wanted to be certain," I say, looking at him and wondering what he is thinking.

The maitre'd shows up with Mason's drink and he orders another double before he downs this drink. The maitre'd looks around the empty dining room before looking at me. I look over at Mason and his eyes are glassy.

I look at the maitre'd who is still standing there. "Bring him one more along with the check, please."

"Certainly."

Mason closes his eyes and leans forward and rests his elbows on his knees again. He runs his fingers across his bottom lip. "Are you having any symptoms? Is that why you took the pregnancy tests?"

"I'm always tired and I felt dizzy a couple of times. I just wanted to clear my thoughts. I wanted us to be able to move on and put all this behind us. I didn't expect the tests to be positive."

The maitre'd arrives at the table and hands Mason his double Scotch and hands me the check. I pay the bar bill with cash while Mason downs this drink, too. He smiles at me and I know he is drunk.

"Would you please have the valet pull the last car around and help me get him to the car?"

"Of course, just give me a minute," the maitre'd says, walking away from the table.

 "Angel?"

"Mason?" I look at him with a sad smile. He is smiling and I know it's from the alcohol.

"You're beautisful," he slurs.

"Come on, Handsome, let's get you home." I pick up the engagement ring, and look at it closely before I place it safely back into the velvet box and put it in my purse. I also toss an additional tip on the table. Maybe that will make up for them staying open later for us.

We walk Mason out and help him get into the passenger seat of his Porsche.

I tip the valet and get into the driver's seat. I think about how the roles have changed. Mason is always the protector and is always so in control; now it's my turn to take care of him.

I look over at Mason, who is resting his head on the back of the seat with his eyes closed. "Buckle up, Handsome," I say, sitting behind the wheel in the driver's seat.

He looks over at me with glassy eyes. "You're driving," he states, and it's not a question. He looks out the window in confusion, before looking over at me again. "I'm drunk."

"I know."

"I'm very drunk." He looks out the window again. "I have never been in the passenger seat of my car before."

"We'll be home very soon.

"Are you buckled in, Beauty?" he slurs.

I smile. "I am, Handsome, we'll be home soon."

I cautiously pull out of the parking lot into the main street. I look at Mason and he is resting his head on back of the seat with his eyes closed. We drive to his beach house in silence. Mason begins to snore as I pull into his garage. I get out and open his car door. I hope he wakes up easily.

"Mason," I say, stroking his cheek lightly. He opens his eyes and smiles at me.

"Hi."

I smile. "Hi, we're home. Let me help you out," I say, reaching my hand in for his.

He tries to swivel in his seat before he unbuckles his seat belt. When he is unable to turn anymore, he laughs. "I'm struck," he slurs.

I laugh, too. "You're stuck?"

"Yeah, I'm struck?"

I reach in and unbuckle his seat belt for him. "There, let's try this again."

Mason turns and stands up. I shut his car door and help him into the house. He stumbles through the house and into the bedroom before he flops down on the bed fully clothed.

"Happy birthsday," he slurs.

I laugh. I think he is already asleep. I remove his shoes and he doesn't move. I walk into the kitchen and get a bottle of water and some Tylenol and set it on his nightstand for when he wakes up. *He is going to need this.* After I cover him with my quilt, I go into the restroom and get ready for bed. I get into my purse and pull out the black velvet box that holds the engagement ring. I open it and look at it and touch it softly. My life with Mason is over before it began; I will never know what the ring will look like on my finger or how perfect my life with Mason may have been. It is beautiful. After I place it back in the box and place the box next to the bottle of water on his nightstand, I go to bed. I scoot as close to Mason as I can. I always sleep better when I feel him next to me.

He turns into me and wraps his arm around me. "Angel?" he whispers.

"I'm here," I say, stroking Mason's cheek.

"Can I be the dad?" he whispers so softly that I almost miss it, before he falls back to sleep.

I stroke his cheek and whisper into his ear, "Oh, Mason, I wouldn't want anyone else to be."

Mason

I wake up and it is still dark outside. My head hurts and my mouth feels like cotton. I look at the cable box — the time reads 3:54 a.m. Angel is lying in the crook of my arm, smelling like peaches and cinnamon. I kiss the top of her head and she rolls over. On the nightstand is a bottle of water and some Tylenol she must have laid out for me. Grateful they are within reach, I take the Tylenol and down the bottle of water. I look on the nightstand and a small black velvet box is sitting there. I reach for it and open it. The engagement ring I bought Angel is still inside. The events of last night come rushing back to me. I close my eyes as I remember: Angel's birthday, the dinner, the proposal, and the pregnancy. *The pregnancy.*

I slowly get out of bed, careful not to wake Angel, and head into the guest bath. I look in the mirror and stare at myself as I remember last night. Did Angel tell me she took three pregnancy tests? Three? What did I say? Fuck, did I order a double Scotch? My head throbs at the memory. How many drinks did I have? Did Angel tell me she was pregnant and I got drunk after hearing the news? *Smooth, Mason.* That is not how I envisioned the night going. I run my hands through my hair and just stare at my reflection in the mirror again. Fuck, did I just think Fuck? I remember that I am supposed to stop cussing to be a better person for her. This is going to be harder than I thought.

I shower and dress for the day, wishing it were the weekend; I sure could use a day off. It's 4:44 a.m. and we both have work today. I make a mental list of what I need to do today before I get home tonight. I set the coffee pot timer for a little before 6:30 for Angel and leave her a note on top of my pillow. I kneel down beside her near the bed and watch her sleep. She is so beautiful. I brush her hair away from her face and kiss her goodbye before heading out the door. She doesn't stir.

Angel

I wake up to my alarm clock at 6:30 a.m. The aroma of coffee is in the air. I turn off the alarm and roll over to wake Mason up. He isn't in bed, but there is a note on top of his pillow. I read it: *Good morning, Beauty. I forgot about an early-morning staff meeting I am having at work. The coffee should be ready for you. I was hoping maybe you could meet me at my office for lunch today? I love you, Mason.* Either he really did have a meeting this morning or he had to get away from me to think about last night. He has never asked me to meet him for lunch before, and he has never left while I was still asleep before either.

I get up and have my coffee first, then shower. I decide on a white blouse with a grey pencil skirt and heels. Sadly, my days of wearing form-fitting clothes are limited. I get dressed and look at myself in the floor-length mirror; I'm happy my outfit still fits. I turn sideways, and I don't look pregnant.

I go into work carrying doughnuts and coffee for Sara, Brea, and me. They are already at their desks working when I get there. My friends warmly greet me.

"I brought breakfast," I say, placing the bag of doughnuts and coffee on the break-room table.

Sara stands, looks in the bag, and is surprised to see doughnuts instead of the muffins that I usually bring.

"First Brea, and now you. If we keep eating these, we are all going to get fat."

Brea stands up from her desk and rubs her big pregnant belly: "Who are you calling fat?"

We all laugh as Brea makes her way over to the table and takes a doughnut from the bag.

"Um, not you." I smile.

"Good, I'm very sensitive about my weight, you know." Brea picks up a vanilla cream fill doughnuts and takes a bite.

"Yeah, we can see that." Sara laughs.

"How was your birthday dinner with Mason last night?" Brea asks.

"It was good; thanks for asking." I take my coffee and head over to my desk. I don't want to go into details about last night with them. I sit at my desk and my phone rings. Grateful for the distraction, I answer it cheerfully.

We are busy until lunchtime. I tell Sara and Brea that I am going to have lunch with Mason at his office. They both brought their lunches to work today and will stay in and eat at the office.

I park my car in the parking lot outside of Mason's office. I have butterflies in my stomach wondering why he wanted to meet me here. He has never asked me to have lunch with him here before. Maybe he wants to end our relationship. Maybe it's too much for him to handle. God, what if he doesn't even remember last night. He was pretty drunk. His car is the only other car in the lot, besides mine. I send him a text and tell him I am outside. Mason opens the back door for me and greets me with a smile.

"Hi, I'm glad you made it." He holds the door open wide for me to walk through.

"We had some down time, so I was able to leave," I say, following him down the hallway and into his office.

"You look beautiful. Please sit," he says, pointing to the brown leather couch, as he closes his office door.

"Thank you and all right." I sit down and Mason sits across from me in one of the big overstuffed cloth chairs.

"Have you eaten yet?"

"No, not yet. I came right over to see you. I'll get something when I leave." Mason seems so formal and it is beginning to scare me. "Is everything all right?"

Mason leans up from the chair and rests his elbows on his knees. "Everything's fine. Carla is bringing us food back so we can have lunch together here before you leave."

"Ok, are you sure you're all right? You seem a little… different."

Mason looks at me with a sad smile. "I wanted to talk to you about last night."

"Mason, look, if this is too much for you, I totally get that. I didn't mean to drop a bomb on you like that. I had no idea you were going to propose to me last night." I start to stand and Mason stops me.

"Don't leave, sit down," he says and I do. I always do what Mason wants. He carries such authority.

"Are you done?" he asks.

"Yes," I say, straightening my skirt and picking at a piece of lint that doesn't exist.

"Good. First of all, I'm sorry about last night. I should have handled things differently."

"Mason, please…"

"Angel, let me talk."

"Ok." It's the only thing I say. Mason is never short with me; I know he has something important to say.

"Last night you told me you took three pregnancy tests. Is that right?"

"Yes."

"Where did you buy them?"

"What difference…"

"Where, Angel?"

"Publix."

"Did you take them all at once or did you wait in between?"

"I took one, waited for the results, and then took another one. I couldn't pee right away so I had to drink some water before I took the last one."

"I see."

"Look, Mason, I don't see what difference it makes about where I bought them or how long I waited to pee in between the tests."

"Angel, what does this say?" he asks, pointing to his nametag, smiling.

I have to smile, too. "It says, Mason Myles."

"Look again, what else does it say?"

Damn him, I know where he's going with this. I lean forward and squint my eyes to make it seem like I can't read the rest of it.

"What else does it say, Angel?"

"It says, Mason Myles, M.D." I smile.

"Very good, do you know why it says M.D. after my name?"

I don't say anything, I just look at him.

"I'll tell you why. I went to medical school for a very long time to get those initials after my name. Believe it or not, I'm a pretty smart man and one thing I know a lot about is medicine."

"Ok, doctor, I get it. What is your point?"

"Angel, my point is, sometimes those tests you buy in the grocery stores, supermarkets, or pharmacies are old and outdated. Sometimes those tests are not accurate or can give a false positive. My point is, maybe it was an old test and maybe, just maybe, it was a false positive."

"Oh God, I never thought about that," I say, leaning back into the couch.

There is a knock at the door. Mason stands and goes to the door to answer it. I don't see anyone, but I can hear him talking to his office manager and friend, Carla. He closes the door and carries the food over and places it on the coffee table.

Mason sits beside me on the couch. He takes my hand in his and says, "Angel, look at me."

I look up at him.

"I would like to get you an accurate pregnancy test; that requires me to draw some blood and send it out to be tested. I want to be positive so we know what our future holds for us."

I just sit there. I hear him, but I don't say anything. There is hope that I may not be pregnant, pregnant with Jim's baby.

When I look at him, he asks, "Would you be willing to take another pregnancy test? I'll send your blood out with an alias listed on it, so no one will know it's you."

"You think maybe those tests were wrong?"

"I don't know," he says, stroking my knuckle with his thumb. "I just want to be 100 percent positive so we know what to expect."

"Of course, I will. Whatever it takes to know, I'll do it."

"That's my girl," Mason smiles. "Let's eat first, then I'll get a blood sample from you."

Mason

I walk Angel out to her car and open her door for her.

"It will take a day or two until we get the results back. There's no need to worry or stress about this until we know the results."

"I know, but it's just so hard."

"Beauty," I say, cupping her cheeks with my hands. "Don't worry about this, we can't change anything by worrying about it, and we'll deal with the news when we get it."

Angel takes a deep breath and leans her cheek into my hand before closing her eyes.

I kiss her forehead and leave my mouth there, "I love you."

"I love you, too."

"I'll meet you at home tonight; buckle up and drive safely. We'll talk more about this then."

"Ok, have a good day at work," she says as she climbs into her SUV.

I watch as Angel pulls out of the parking lot before I run my hands through my hair. This is going to be a stressful couple days. I don't want her to worry so I'll do what I need to do to plaster a believable smile to my face.

I head inside and ask Carla to call the lab company to pick up the stat lab draws. I know it's early, but I want them sent out as soon as possible. Usually they pick up the labs at the end of the day, but I don't want to wait any longer than I have to.

Carla doesn't ask me any questions, and I wouldn't expect her to. She is an excellent office manager. She calls the lab for an early pick-up, and I return to my office to get ready to see more patients.

I arrive at home and am surprised to see Angel is already there. I walk into the house and the aroma of Italian food hits me immediately. Chicken Parmesan and pasta. Angel has her back to me as she stands at the stove. She is still so easily startled; I clear my throat before walking further into the kitchen.

"It smells delicious in here," I say, walking up behind her and wrapping my arms around her.

"Thank you. I thought I would make your favorite … well, one of your favorite meals."

"That was thoughtful. What's the special occasion?" I ask, wrapping my arm around her and kissing the top of her head.

"Just because I think you are wonderful and the best thing that has ever happened to me." She turns around and steps away from the stove, before standing on her tiptoes to kiss me.

I lift her up off the floor and she squeals. I laugh. "Well, I think you are pretty amazing yourself," I say, kissing her back.

I set her down gently until her feet are on the ground. "Do I have time to shower first?"

"You have about 20 minutes."

"Perfect."

"Do you want to eat in here or outside tonight?"

I look outside and see that the tide is going out. "How about we eat outside, then we can walk on the beach and look for sea treasures, since it's low tide?" Angel calls seashells, sea rocks, sharks' teeth, and sand dollars, sea treasures. Well, anything that comes from the ocean is considered a sea treasure when it comes to Angel.

"Oh, that sounds great. I have a glass vase that needs to be filled up with seashells," she says, excitedly.

"All right, just give me 20 minutes and I'll be ready to eat," I say, walking into the master bedroom.

After dinner I help Angel clear the table and help her clean up the kitchen. Once everything is put away and cleaned up, Angel grabs two Baggies from the drawer and hands one to me.

"Here, this is for your sea treasures."

"Thank you," I say, taking the Baggie from her.

I take her hand in mine and we walk on the beach. Angel picks up seashells and rocks and puts them in her Baggie. I find a few sharks' teeth and place them in my Baggie.

"You're good at finding sharks' teeth. I have never been able to find one on my own."

"It's because you don't know what to look for."

"What do you mean?"

I stop near a pile of seashells and let go of Angel's hand.

"What do you see?" I ask, while looking down at the pile of shells.

Angel looks down at the pile of seashells and frowns. "I see some broken seashells."

"Yes, but what else do you see?"

She looks at the pile again with furrowed brows.

"Beauty, look beyond the broken shells."

Angel looks at the seashells and kicks a few shells around with her feet. She smiles and bends down to pick something up. She stands and holds two sharks' teeth in her hands.

"Look," she smiles, "I found some."

"Very good, now you know what to look for." I take her hand and we turn back towards the beach house.

"Thank you, Mason."

I smile and say, "You're welcome, Beauty."

"Hey, I was thinking that we should go to church on Sunday," Angel says, while looking up at me.

"I think that is a great idea," I say, looking down at her.

"You do?"

"I do. Do you have a church that you go to?"

"No." She frowns.

"We could find one together or we could go to the church that I went to as a child. Mom and Dad still go there. It's not a Catholic Church, though."

"Sounds perfect. God is God, and I don't believe it matters what church or building you're in to worship him."

"Angel, that is very touching," I say, swinging her arm. "I believe the same thing. God is God no matter where we are, or what religion we are."

"Good, we have a date."

"What?" I ask.

"A date, we have a date for church on Sunday," she says, smiling.

"Yes, Beauty, we do."

We walk the rest of the way home talking about her pregnancy test results. We decide that when they come in, I'll have them placed in a sealed envelope and we will find out the results together, at home. I omit telling her I put a stat order on them and we will have the results tomorrow. We'll deal with the news of the pregnancy tomorrow.

I drop Angel off at work this morning and tell her I'll pick her up at 5:00. I go in to work and tell Carla that when the results come in for Mrs. Ana Rose to place the report in an envelope and leave it on my desk, in my office, for me. I decided on that name, Ana Rose, after Angel's mother and aunt. I make a conscious effort to avoid my office throughout the day. I don't want to see the envelope and I don't want to know when the results arrive. I call Angel at lunchtime and ask her whether she wants to order takeout for dinner. Angel is so easy to please. It doesn't matter to her what we do or where we go. She is just as happy to stay at home as she is to go out. Sometimes I think she prefers just staying in.

At the end of the day, I walk into my office and see an envelope lying on my desk. I pick it up and look at it. It is marked "Mrs. Ana Rose." I place the envelope in my pocket and take my keys from inside my desk drawer. I call in an order for dinner at Fast and Fresh Deli before leaving to pick up Angel.

During the drive home, she tells me about the new updates on Brea and Vincent's wedding. They have the caterer lined up and the wedding party has all accepted. They also have the venue and the bakery secured. She talks excitedly about the wedding shower she and Sara are planning for Brea.

Brea and Vincent's wedding is just over three months away and the baby is due in less than three months. Not great planning to have the wedding so soon after the arrival of their baby, but Vincent said he is already on his honeymoon. *Lucky bastard.* Must be nice to know what direction your life is going and who will be in it. I am happy for him, but sometimes I feel envious of his good fortune in finding happiness with Brea.

Angel and I arrive home, and I shower before dinner. After working all day and seeing patients with different types of illnesses, I don't want to take a chance of bringing something home to Angel.

After dinner I take a deep breath and tell Angel her results came back. I see her face fall. I remove the envelope from my back pocket and hold it out for her. She looks at me — her eyes are filling up with tears.

"I'm scared of what's in there," she says, not reaching for the envelope.

"Angel, there's nothing to be scared of. Either you'll have the same result when you took the test, or you won't. If the results are different, then you can put all this behind you."

"But, what if they aren't different? What if I am really pregnant with Jim's baby? Then what … then what will happen with me, with us?" Angel begins to cry.

"Angel, don't cry," I say, pulling her into me. I hold her tightly and stroke her long curly hair. She returns the hug and lays her head on my shoulder. She smells like peaches and cinnamon. I inhale her and she laughs.

"Why are you laughing?" I ask, moving my mouth side to side on top of her head. Her hair is so soft against my lips.

"Because you always smell me."

"It's because you always smell so good."

Angel leans back with tears in her eyes and takes a deep breath.

"Ok, I'm ready. Will you open it?"

Angel

My lips begin to quiver as Mason starts to open the envelope holding the results of my pregnancy test. I know when I told him I was pregnant that he didn't handle it very well. He had proposed to me on my birthday, then I told him I was pregnant. I think he was in shock; he started ordering shots — not just shots, but double shots. He got drunk faster than I have ever seen anyone get drunk. I know if the results are still positive, he won't be able to handle it again.

"Wait!" I say, before he opens the folded paper in his hand.

"What is it?" Mason asks, startled.

I stand up and go to the bar. I get the bottle of Scotch and set it on the coffee table in front of him. He looks up at me with a raised brow.

"Just in case," I say, sitting back down beside Mason.

"Angel has jokes."

"No, no jokes. I just want to be prepared," I say, sitting back down beside Mason.

"Ready?"

"Ready," I say, holding my hands to my stomach. I feel like I'm going to get sick.

"I love you," he says, smiling.

"I love you, too," I smile back.

Mason opens the folded paper and we both look at it. My heart falls into my stomach. I look up at Mason and he is expressionless. He is still looking at the results. It must be a talent all doctors have, or maybe they have to take a class to be able to look expressionless while giving bad news.

Mason looks over at me with a sad smile. He puts the paper on the table next to the bottle of Scotch and looks over at me again. He places his hands on my cheeks and wipes my tears away.

"This doesn't change anything."

I lean my face into his hand and close my eyes. "Mason, I'm pregnant. This changes everything."

"Angel, this doesn't change anything with us. I love you."

I stand up to put some distance between Mason and me. I need to talk seriously to him, and being so close to him makes that difficult to do sometimes.

"Mason, this isn't fair. This isn't fair for you. You didn't ask for any of this."

"Angel?" Mason starts to stand.

I hold my hand out to stop him. "No, please let me finish."

"All right." He sits back down and puts one arm over the back of the couch and rests his other arm on the arm of the couch.

"Mason, this isn't fair to you. We haven't even made love yet and now I'm pregnant. What will we tell people, tell our friends and family?" I pace back and forth without looking at Mason. I don't want to look into his eyes. I don't want to see his pain. "This could ruin your reputation. People will think you got your girlfriend pregnant. They'll think you're careless and irresponsible." I look over at him, "Do you know what this could do to your medical practice? People won't want to go to see a doctor who is careless and reckless."

"Angel..."

"Mason, I'm not done," I say, "I have issues with this." I sit across from him and lean forward so I am not slouched into the chair. Mason imitates my pose on the couch that he is sitting on. I begin to cry. "Mason, I'm not even sure I can love this baby. This baby's father is a rapist and he tried to kill me. How will I be able to love this child? What if every time I look at it, I see Jim? Mason, what if I'm unable to love this baby?"

I hold my stomach and run into the restroom. I know this isn't morning sickness although I couldn't keep my dinner down. This is me coming to terms with reality. I have had thoughts about not being able to love this baby many times, but I have never spoken the words aloud. Mason probably thinks I am some terrible person for thinking them. There is no way he will be able to relate to my confusion. I look in the mirror and I hardly recognize the person looking back at me. I am disgusted by the person I have become. I splash cold water on my face and head out into the living room, where I left Mason sitting on the couch with a bottle of Scotch in front of him.

Mason isn't in the room and I look at the bottle of Scotch, thinking it should be empty by now. The bottle sits on the coffee table untouched. *He didn't turn to alcohol this time. He must be accepting this better than I am.*

I look outside and Mason is standing on the lanai watching me. I stand there and I just look at him. He is leaning against the railing, looking handsome. He is wearing a pair of plaid shorts and a white linen shirt. His hair is curly and unruly; his eyes are dark and unreadable. He smiles and pushes off from the railing. He walks slowly into the house and stands in front of me. Mason touches my cheeks with his hands and kisses me tenderly. I kiss him back.

"Angel, sit down," he says, once our kiss ends, and I do. I always do what Mason tells me to do. I know he would never do anything that would hurt me. Once I am seated, I look up and Mason smiles down at me.

Mason kneels down in front of me and takes my left hand in his. My belly does somersaults.

"You are so beautiful," he says, while stroking my fingers. "Angel, I love you and I want to be with you. The news we received today changes nothing."

"Mason?"

"Angel, it's my turn to talk."

"Oh, all right," I whisper and force my mouth closed. I want to say something, but I need to let Mason have his say, first.

"Beauty, when I first met you I knew you were like no other woman in the world. I knew I had to get to know you and I was right. You are truly like no other. I love you and I want to be with you, forever. You make me want to be a better person, you make me want to see the world through your innocent eyes. You make me want to protect you, care for you, and love you, with everything that I am as a man." Mason reaches into his pants pocket and pulls out the engagement ring and holds it to my ring finger. "Angel, the news we received today doesn't change that. It doesn't change the way I feel for you, care for you, or love you. I want to be your husband, I want to be the father of your children, and I want us to grow old together. I want to be the father to this baby: *our* baby." Mason looks me in the eyes and smiles, his beautiful, dimpled, and genuine smile, "Angelica Hope Ramos Perez, will you *please* marry me?"

"Really?" I cry, with shaky hands and blurred vision. The tears are streaming down my face. "You want me to marry you and you want to be this baby's father?"

"Yes, really, I do," Mason says, still holding the ring to my finger with a smile. "I want that more than anything I have ever wanted in my life."

"Mason, how do you know you can love this baby?"

"Beauty, this baby is part of you and I already love it. I promise to love you and this baby like I have never loved or cared for anything in my life."

"Yes," I squeal, "Mason Alexander Myles, I would love to marry you."

Mason slides the ring on my finger and it is a perfect fit. He lifts me from the couch, and I stand on my tiptoes to kiss him. He picks me up until we are eye to eye. I can feel the smile on his lips during our kiss. I wrap my legs around him and he leans his head back away from me, smiling. I can't help but smile, too.

"We are getting married," he states. "You will be mine, forever. Just like I knew you would be," he adds before kissing me again.

"Oh, my God, I need to call Uncle Raùl and Aunt Maria and tell them about the engagement. They will be so upset with me for not telling them."

"It's all right, Beauty. Raùl already knows and I'm sure Maria knows, too. I called and asked his permission last week before I asked you. He is probably wondering what is taking me so long. He thought I was going to ask you on your birthday. You may want to call him and tell him I got cold feet or something."

"You called my uncle and asked his permission to marry me?"

"I did, why?"

"Do people still do that?"

"Well, I have never done this before, but yes, I believe that is the proper way and the right thing to do. If it were my daughter, I would want the person to ask my permission, first."

"And that is why I love you," I say, kissing him again.

"It's not because of my good looks and charm?" He smiles.

"Well, it's that, too," I laugh.

"Go call them. I'm sure he is waiting to hear from you."

Mason gently puts me on the floor. I reach for my cell phone and call my aunt and uncle about the news of our engagement. They are both excited and they love Mason. Maria asks questions like when the wedding is, where the wedding will be, and things like that. Questions that I have no answers to. Uncle Raùl asks to speak to Mason before we hang up. We say our goodbyes and I hand the phone over to Mason so they can talk. Mason smiles and says, "Thank you," before hanging up after talking to my uncle.

"My turn," Mason says, while taking his cell phone out of his pocket to call someone. Mason calls his Mom and Dad, and I can hear screaming on the other end of the phone. He laughs, then hands me the phone. His mother, Lilly, is screaming with excitement. They both congratulate me before I hand the phone back over to him.

"Should I call Sara and Brea and tell them?" I ask.

"Do you want to?"

"I'm feeling a little overwhelmed; I think I want to get ready for bed. Is that all right with you?"

"Me, too. You can tell them tomorrow at work."

Mason

Angel and I get ready for bed, and she lies in the crook of my arm. She holds her hand up in the air and looks at her engagement ring. "This is so beautiful," she says, while staring at the ring.

"It's even more beautiful on your hand."

Angel turns her head and looks up at me, "You always say the nicest things."

I bend down to kiss the tip of her nose. "I always speak the truth and that is the truth."

"I love you," she says, cuddling back into my arm.

"I love you, more, Beauty. Do you have any idea how long you want this engagement to be, or where you would like the wedding to be held, or..."

"Oh, are you in a hurry to get married since I'm pregnant?" she asks, sitting up and resting against the headboard. "We can hurry it up if you want."

"No, I was trying to find out what you wanted. We can get married this weekend or next year. I don't want a two- or three-year engagement, though. I love you and I want you to be Mrs. Myles as soon as I can."

"I love the way that sounds. Do you have any ideas about when or where?"

"Um, yes, I guess I do. I didn't expect you to ask me for my opinion, though."

"Why not?" Angel asks, reaching over for a tablet and pen from the nightstand.

"Because most girls already have an idea of what they want for their wedding day."

Angel leans back into the headboard and looks at me. "I'm not like most girls."

I smile, "No, you sure aren't."

"Ideas?" she asks, holding the pen to the paper.

"Well, I think we need to wait until after Brea and Vincent's wedding to have *our* wedding. We don't want to interfere with their wedding."

"Good point," she taps the pen to paper. "So any time after October 23rd."

"You will be due when... around February? We won't know for sure until you see a doctor."

"February? If everything goes right, it'll be a Valentine's baby."

"Well, yes, assuming everything does go right. It will be right around that time."

"So when would we get married? New Year's?" she asks, looking over at me.

"Yes, I was thinking New Year's Eve. We can get married and start our new life together at the beginning of the New Year."

"At your parents' house, down by the water, at midnight?"

"Yes, I was thinking the same thing. We can have just our family and friends. Small and intimate..."

"Just the way I like it," she smiles and leans into me.

I wrap my arms around her, "Just the way you like it, Beauty, small and intimate."

"Do you think they'll agree to have it there?"

"I think they will argue with us if we don't have it there."

She places the pen and paper back on the nightstand.

"I love you," she says, snuggling into me.

I reach over and turn off the lights, "I love you, more."

I wake up for work and Angel is already out of bed. I look into the bathroom and the light is off. I walk out into the kitchen and I can smell bacon cooking.

"You're up pretty early this morning," I say, walking over to the coffee pot to pour me a cup, after kissing her good morning.

"Yes, well, I couldn't sleep."

"Oh, are you feeling all right?" I ask, pouring myself a cup of coffee.

"Just a lot on my mind, that's all," she says, while flipping the bacon over.

I look over and Angel has her notebook and pen lying out on the kitchen island.

"We're going to have to start keeping decaffeinated coffee in the house."

Angel holds up a glass of milk. "I know. I'm going to miss my caffeine in the mornings."

"Are you coming up with some ideas for the wedding?" I ask, nodding towards the pen and paper on the island.

"Pre-wedding things, more like it, a lot of things have been running through my mind. I don't want to forget anything."

"Like what?" I say, sitting at the bar and watching her.

"Like, I think it's time I start looking for office space for my Interior Design business. I would really like to get that started. I'll be taking time off work and I don't think it will be fair to Sara or Brea." Angel turns the bacon over again and pours some scrambled eggs in a frying pan. "And we have other homes that we own. We need to discuss what we are going to do with those. Right now, they are just sitting empty and that is a waste of money and I'm going to need to find a doctor."

"Wow, you didn't get much rest last night, I see."

"No, I guess I didn't, but I feel fine."

I walk over and butter the toast while she places the scrambled eggs and bacon on the plates.

"Let's eat and we can try to resolve some of your dilemmas, shall we?"

"Do you think it's that easy?"

I follow her to the bar and I take the seat across from her.

"Dilemma number one: finding you a doctor. I know a few obstetricians but I can also ask around at work today to see whom people use and whom they like. I can ask some of the patients whom they have used. That way the staff doesn't get suspicious," I say.

"Really? It will be that easy?"

"I hope so. When someone has a good doctor, they love to share it. Believe it or not, it's hard to find a good doctor. You have to like them, trust them, and be able to tell them all kinds of personal things. You have to trust them with your most personal problems."

"Ok, sounds good. I'll also bring up a conversation with Brea to see who they use. I don't think we should announce the pregnancy just yet. We need to make sure we are out of the 'danger zone,'" she says, using air quotation marks.

"I agree, we don't want to announce it too soon. And when we do, we'll announce that it's mine."

"I want to, yes, but some people will know the truth."

"If they aren't family or close friends, they won't know any different."

"Mason, you know I love you, right?"

"I do, and I also know you are going to be Mrs. Mason Myles in the near future."

"I like the way that sounds."

"Me, too. From here on out, I want this baby to be referred to as *my* baby. No more Jim. This baby is *our* baby, mine and yours, got it?"

"Yes, Mason, I got it and I love you."

"Good, I love you, too. Dilemma number two: office space. I think you should work from home. We have empty rooms here you can use. You can set up your office in one of them. Eventually, I want to fill this house up with babies. But until then, you could borrow one of their rooms," I say, taking a sip of my coffee and trying not to smile.

"Babies? How many babies are you talking?" she asks, with a raised brow.

"We can start off with one and stop when all the bedrooms are full."

"Mason, you own a five-bedroom house."

"I know and we occupy only one of those bedrooms."

"Mason, that leaves four other bedrooms."

"I know, I can count." I laugh. *Now would be a good time to change the subject.* "Dilemma number three: extra homes."

"We have two other homes that are sitting vacant. I think we should decide what we are going to do with them. It's a waste of money to pay for them to sit empty. We could be saving the money we are spending to keep them. And don't think I forgot about the baby — make that babies — comment," Angel says, smiling.

"All right, we'll revisit the baby — make that babies — conversation at a later date. Good point on the homes; they are just sitting empty and that is costly. Your cottage was a gift to you from your aunt, right? Aunt Rosie?" I ask.

"Yes, Uncle Raùl's sister."

"Why not re-gift the cottage to him and Maria? It will give them a place to stay when they are in town and it will also remain in the family. Maybe one day, they'll decide to retire here."

"Mason Alexander, that is a wonderful idea. You are so much more than good looks and charm. Who knew that you were also brilliant?" She laughs. "That would be so great if they would move here. I miss them so much."

"I know you do. Who knows what the future holds? Maybe one day they'll decide to make Florida their home."

"Do you believe that?"

"I believe they love you and if they could be closer to you, they would."

"I hope so."

"Oh, I forgot to tell you that I am meeting Madison for lunch today," Mason says.

"I haven't seen her in a long time. We should invite her over for dinner."

"I can do that. I'll invite her over next weekend. I can also ask her to list the condo for us with her real estate company. Maybe she can put it on the market to see if anyone is interested. The economy and real estate are getting better. This might be a good time to list it."

"Mason, you love the condo. I didn't mean for you to sell it. I don't want you to get rid of it because of me."

"No, you're right, it has been sitting empty. I loved it when I bought it, but my life has changed since then." I look over at her and smile. "It's not really a family home. I want something our kids can run around in and I won't be in fear of something happening to them."

Angel looks around the house and smiles. "This is going to be a great family home for our children."

"I think so, too." I look around the house before taking our plates into the kitchen. "I need to shower; I'll use the guest shower and you use the master," I say, looking at Angel.

"I'll hurry so we aren't late."

"Take your time, we still have plenty of time," I say, trying to sound cheerful.

"Ok," she says while walking away from me.

I shower and finish loading the dishwasher when Angel enters the room. She looks beautiful. She is wearing a black knee-length dress and black heels. Her hair is down, curly, and still wet.

"You look beautiful."

She smiles and walks over to me and kisses me, "Thank you, are you ready?"

"I am, do you have everything you need?"

"Yup, lead the way, Handsome."

I drive Angel to work. Sara and Brea are already there when we arrive.

"Want to come in and tell them about our engagement?"

"I can't wait," I say, smiling.

I get out of the car and walk over to Angel's side to open her door for her. I reach my hand in and she takes it and smiles. We walk into the office hand in hand; both of us are smiling. The bell over the door rings, alerting Sara and Brea, who smile when they see us.

"Good morning, everyone." I smile.

Brea walks over and says, "I didn't realize you were starting work here today, Mason?" She laughs.

"Ha, ha, very funny. I'm not. Angel and I have some news we wanted to share with you both."

They both stare at Angel then me. Angel raises her hand and wiggles her ring finger back and forth, drawing attention to the ring there. They both squeal and scream and run over and hug Angel to the point I'm afraid they may hurt her. I back away from the interaction among them.

"I need to get going,"

"Mason, I forgot all about you. Congratulations," Brea says, standing on her tiptoes to hug me.

"Thank you, and that's ok. Have you always been this short?" I say, leaning down to hug her.

"Shut up, Vincent won't let me wear my heels until after the baby's born." She pouts. "He's afraid I'll trip and fall, or topple over from the excess weight; I'm not sure which."

"I can understand that; no man wants to see potential harm done to their child, or their girl."

"What did you just say?"

"Nothing, I was just agreeing with him, that's all."

"Umm mmm."

Sara comes over and hugs me next. I bend down to hug her. "It took you long enough. Donovan said you were going to propose on her birthday," she says, hugging me, so no one else can hear.

"Cold feet," I lie.

"Well, better late than never. Congratulations," she says, kissing me on my cheek.

"Thank you."

"I need to go," I say, walking to the door.

Angel walks with me and kisses me goodbye. "I love you."

"I love you. I'll pick you up right after work."

"Be careful."

I head into work, thankful that it's Friday. I look at the appointment book and notice the last patient is scheduled for 2:00 p.m. I may be able to leave early and run a few errands before I need to pick up Angel after work. I make a list of things I need to do after work and stuff it in my pocket.

I start to see patients and break only for lunch. I check my phone and there is a text from Angel.

A: Mr. Myles, I hope you have a great lunch date with your sister. Thinking of you. I love you, Miss Perez.

M: Miss Perez, soon you will be Mrs. Myles and I can't wait for that day. I also hope you have a great lunch and please eat healthy. My baby likes fruits and vegetables with each meal. Dr. Mason Myles.

A: You're going to make me cry. I love you.

M: I'm sorry, don't cry. Have a good lunch and I love you, too.

Madison and I have lunch next door at the Fast and Fresh Deli. I tell her that Angel and I got engaged and I would like to put the condo up for sale.

"Oh my God, Mason. Do you know how many times a week I get asked about condos in your building? A penthouse with your view, my commission will be through the roof."

"Then it should sell quickly at a good price."

"Wait, I thought you loved it there?"

"I do, but with Angel and me getting married, we need only a family home. The condo was great for a bachelor pad, but it won't do for a family."

"Please tell me, she isn't pregnant?"

"Madison, stop it. We are just planning ahead. The real estate market is going up, and this is prime property. We should be able to get a good price out of it."

We order our lunch and talk about having her over for dinner next week.

"I'll clear my personal things out of the condo this weekend, and if you can, you should try to sell it furnished. Try to get it on the market next week." I swear that I can see dollar signs in Madison's eyes.

"Sounds good, I'll need your key. You have a spare, right?"

"I do, and Madison, I want the best price you can get me."

"I will. I'm good at what I do, so you have nothing to worry about."

"I know I don't. Here's the spare key."

Angel

Mason leaves for work, and Sara, Brea, and I have a difficult time getting into work mode. We talk about Brea and Vincent's wedding and the completion date of their new home. Their home should be completed in another month. They have already started shopping for baby furniture and other essential items they'll need for the baby. Once they move into the new house, the baby will be due in a little over a month.

We also talk about Sara and Donovan's new living arrangements. Sara is very excited with the progression of their relationship and mentions that they both will make a great aunt and uncle to Brea and Vincent's baby. She says that they have also started to baby-proof their house and are buying a few baby items to keep at their home for when the baby visits. Donovan went out and bought electrical outlet covers for the house — believe it or not, when babies are old enough to crawl, they explore things with all their senses and will so such things as lick electrical outlets — and she says that he also cleared out all the cleaning supplies from under the cabinets and moved them out to the garage to a top shelf. I think that is so sweet and a great idea. I think we need to do that, and I also think of how blessed my baby will be to be surrounded by people like them.

They ask me if Mason and I have any plans for a wedding date, and I tell them we were thinking about this year on New Year's Eve. They are excited and think that is a great time to get married and to start over. To finally leave the past in the past. I agree, it is a perfect time to do that. The beginning of a new year and a new life together. I don't want to talk much about our wedding because I don't want to take anything from Brea's wedding. There will be plenty of time to talk about and plan our wedding later.

We finally dive into work and stop only when there is a food delivery. Donovan had soup and salads delivered for everyone from Sweet Tomato's Salads and Soups. Brea and I dig right into the food while Sara leaves the room to call Donovan.

After lunch we work non-stop until quitting time. Mason texts me and tells me he'll be outside when I'm ready. Sara, Brea, and I lock up and walk out of the office together. Mason is leaning against his car and looking handsome when we reach the parking lot.

"Hi," I say, walking over to him.

Mason pushes off from the car and walks over to meet us. "Hi, yourself."

"Don't mind us," Brea says, laughing.

"Hello, Brea and Sara."

"Have a good night, Mason and Angel," Sara says, getting into her car.

"Good night and drive safely," Mason says, waving her goodbye.

Mason walks over and opens Brea's car door for her. He stands beside the car while she gets in and buckles up. I watch them interact, and I see when he places his hand on her belly. He waits only a few moments and they both smile. He waves as she backs up and then he walks over to me.

"I missed you."

I wrap my arms around his neck and kiss him. "I missed you, too."

"Ready to head home?" he asks, while walking with me to the car. "We need to get the groceries put away."

"You went to the grocery store?"

"I finished with my last patient early so I had some extra time." Mason opens my car door for me and waits for me to get in.

"I didn't realize we were low on groceries."

"We're not, now buckle up," he says, while shutting my car door. He gets in and buckles his own seat belt, smiling.

I look in the back seat of the car and see that it is full of grocery bags. "If we weren't low on groceries, then what is all that?" I ask as he pulls out into the main road.

Mason looks over at me still smiling, then looks into the back seat. "Just some extras I thought we needed until grocery day on Sunday."

"It looks like more than extras."

Mason and I drive to the beach house, and he tells me he made an appointment at an OB/GYN for me for next Friday. He also adds that he found the perfect doctor in Sarasota for me. The daughter of one of his patients is seeing her, and the mother swears by the doctor's work. He tells me that is good enough for him. If it's good enough for Mason, then it's good enough for me. I also notice the doctor is a female, although I don't say anything.

We arrive at the beach house. As usual, I stay seated and wait for Mason to open my car door for me. I reach in to get some bags from the back seat when Mason asks that I check the mail instead. Mason on occasion can be very overprotective and it is very sexy. I love overprotective Mason. Usually this happens when a lot of people are around and when he fears for my safety, like when Jim was alive. Now Mason is in overprotective mode because I am pregnant. He probably doesn't even know he does it.

By the time I get the few pieces of mail from the mailbox, Mason already has everything gathered in his hands and is waiting for me.

"Do you want me to take some of those bags from you?"

"No, I have them. Would you mind closing the car door, please?"

"No, of course not."

I follow Mason into the house, closing the doors and locking up behind us. I help him unload all the groceries and I am in awe over all the fresh produce and organic foods he bought. Before I have a chance to say anything, Mason reaches into a bag and removes an item, then walks into the bedroom with it. Thinking it must be a personal hygiene item, I continue my quest to get everything put away.

When I am done, I grab a cranberry juice and head outside to the lanai. I know Mason is already in the shower. It's the first thing he does when he gets home. I swear, if his office had a shower in it, he would shower there, before coming home. Mason is so afraid of bringing germs from the office into our home. He always showers before and after work, and sometimes he showers before bed. It's no wonder he smells so good all the time.

He walks out into the lanai, carrying a beer. I kick out the seat across from me for him to sit down.

"Are you tired tonight, Miss Angel?" Mason laughs.

"I am, Mr. Myles. I worked hard today."

"You did? Is it too much for you?" he asks, concerned.

"Mason, I sit on my butt and answer phones all day. Do you really think I work hard?" I ask.

"Well, I did, until you put it that way."

We both laugh.

Mason reaches for my hand and kisses it.

"So, I take it you thought we needed some fresh fruits and vegetables in the house, huh?"

"I told you my baby likes fresh fruits and vegetables. I just wanted to make sure *she* has enough to eat."

"How do you know it's a *she* and how do you know *it* likes fruits and veggies? Maybe *it* likes Snickers and Pepsi?" I grin.

"Well, maybe it's not a girl, I'll give you that. But fruits and veggies are definitely good for mom and my baby — and me. We can all benefit from eating healthier."

"You're right about that, Mason."

"Why, thank you."

"Hey, I wanted to talk to you about what I said last night."

Mason turns his chair towards me to give me his undivided attention. "Ok, it sounds serious."

I clear my throat and sit up a little straighter in my chair. "Last night, I said some pretty ugly things about this baby, that maybe I wouldn't be able to love it."

"Beauty?"

"No, please, let me finish. I need to say this."

"All right," Mason sits back in his chair, never taking his eyes off mine. "Go on."

"Mason, last night I said some things that I didn't mean. I said some things out of fear, and I never should have spoken those words." I look at him so he can see I am serious. "I didn't look at the whole picture, and I never should have thought those things. I'm sorry." I lean forward in my chair. "I know I probably sounded like a monster, and that isn't who or what I am. I just want you to know that."

"May I talk, now?"

"Yes, please."

Mason leans up and takes my hand in his. "Beauty, you don't need to explain anything. The things you were feeling are normal for anyone who has been through what you have been through." Mason touches my engagement ring and smiles. "I know you will be a great mother and will love this baby with every fiber in your being, because *that* is the person that you are."

"Mason, how can you be so sure? You always have so much faith in me."

"Angel, I know your heart and I know who you are. You have fears and that is normal. You have been through hell and back, but you came out stronger than ever."

"God, your faith in me is astounding. I don't deserve you."

"No, Beauty, you don't. You deserve so much more."

Mason

Angel and I wait in the waiting room of her OB/GYN appointment. I made the appointment first thing in the morning so I wouldn't have to miss a whole day of work. Angel, on the other hand, took the entire day off. She wasn't sure how she would feel after the appointment.

Angel has been drinking water for the last forty-five minutes. She needs to have a full bladder when they do the ultrasound. I feel anxious, but I am more relaxed than Angel is. She is fidgeting with her nails and biting the inside of her cheek.

"Doesn't that hurt?"

She looks up at me with a raised brow. "Does what hurt?"

I take her hand in mine. "Biting the inside of your cheek."

"Oh, I guess not. I didn't even realize I was doing that."

"You do that when you're anxious."

"I'm not anxious," she lies.

I look around the waiting room, which is full of expectant mothers and scared boyfriends and husbands. All the women are in various stages of pregnancy. A nurse calls a name, and a very pregnant woman waddles along with her husband through the door.

"That doesn't make you anxious?" I ask, smiling.

"What, that woman who is about to deliver at any minute?"

"Yeah, her."

"Yeah, it makes me a lot anxious. She's going to push a human being out of an opening the size of a nostril. That scares me to death."

I look at Angel and she is biting the inside of her cheek again.

"You're going to draw blood, if you don't stop, and it's not the size of a nostril." I lift her hand to my lips and kiss it.

"I'm sorry, I don't even know I'm doing it, and it's not much bigger than a nostril."

"It stretches. You have nothing to be afraid of." I intertwine our fingers and smile.

"I wish I could be as calm as you. Are you medicated or something?"

I laugh. "No medication. I just know there isn't anything to be afraid of," I lie.

I'm glad Angel doesn't know how I really feel. I am scared right along with her.

"I have to pee."

"Hopefully, it won't be much longer."

"Miss Perez," a nurse calls from the open doorway.

Angel and I stand, and I reach for her hand while we walk towards the nurse. We are greeted warmly, and then they check her weight and give her a paper gown to put on. Angel sits on the bed fidgeting while I take the seat next to her.

"Do you want something to read while we wait?"

"No, I'm fine. I didn't realize how anxious I would be today. It's one appointment. I shouldn't be worried."

"You're right, Angel. It's one appointment, and there isn't anything to worry about."

"Do you ever get excited about anything?"

"Nope, I have nerves of steel." I laugh.

"Nerves of steel, huh?"

Just then, the doctor comes into the room and introduces herself as Doctor Rosa Thomas. She talks to Angel about her family medical history, and asks me about mine. Before I give any health information about me, we inform the doctor that the baby is the result of a rape and the father's health history is unknown. I inform her we would like to keep this between us and I will be listed as the baby's father on all the paperwork.

I hold Angel's hand and smile at her. I don't want her to dwell on the past. This is my baby, and I dare anyone to say otherwise.

"I understand and I'm sorry. Go ahead and lie back. I want to listen to the baby's heartbeat and measure your belly. I also want to get an ultrasound and see the baby's organs and make sure they are functioning properly. It'll be too soon to tell the gender of the baby, so don't get your hopes up. Once we are done, I'll be able to give you an estimated due date."

Angel lies back and I stand next to her. My hands begin to feel sweaty, and my heart starts to beat a little faster. Nerves of steel, my ass, I'm a nervous wreck. I am grateful that Angel can't tell.

"Are you all right?" Angel asks, sweetly.

I look down at her and she is looking at me, concerned. I look over at the doctor, who is also looking at me.

"I'm fine, why?" Not sure why they are both staring at me.

"Because you look pale."

I take a deep breath and smile before saying, "Beauty, I'm fine." I stroke her cheek with my free hand and continue holding her hand with my other hand. Touching her always calms me.

The doctor dims the lights, and Angel and I both watch as the doctor gels Angel's belly and moves the wand side to side. We hear a swishing sound first, and then a heartbeat.

Angel squeezes my hand and I smile at her. The doctor moves the wand back and forth and then higher and lower.

"Let's take a look," the doctor says, as she turns on the monitor. The monitor comes to life and reveals a grainy image of a peanut shape. The swishing sound returns and is mixed with a very fast heartbeat. The doctor points out the heart, and tells us the peanut shape is the baby. I squeeze Angel's hand and bend down to whisper in her ear.

"Our baby is beautiful." Angel looks at me and she is crying.

I kiss her cheek — it is wet. I reach over and grab the box of tissues from the counter before handing a few to Angel.

"Thank you."

I don't say anything; I just watch the monitor. The fast heartbeat is mixed with more swishing sounds. I become a little more anxious, and I take some deep breaths to try to calm me.

"Is everything all right?" Angel asks, with a shaky voice.

"Everything's fine and the baby looks healthy," the doctor says.

Angel looks at me and I smile.

"That's great news," I say, never taking my eyes off the screen.

Doctor Thomas prints off a couple pictures before turning off the monitor. She turns the lights back on in the room and Angel quickly wipes away her tears. I know Angel's mind is spinning like crazy. The doctors pulls something out from her pocket and turns the dials. She rechecks her chart and readjusts the dial again.

"This little pocket calculator tells me that you will be due on February 6th. That makes you about 11 weeks. We'll see you in one month and then we'll do another ultrasound."

"I should start to show very soon?"

"Yes, Angel, you will. I recommend that my patients wait until after three months before announcing their pregnancy.

There is always a risk for miscarriage the first trimester. Before you ask, there isn't anything you can do to prevent a miscarriage. Miscarriages are nature's way of aborting unhealthy fetuses. Just take it easy, no heavy lifting, get plenty of rest when you can. It's also too soon to know the sex of the baby. Around five months, we'll have a better chance of finding out the sex. Do either of you have any questions?"

"Um, I have a question. Can we have sex or should we refrain from it? "

"It is fine and very healthy for you and your baby if you want to continue a healthy sexual lifestyle. As long as you feel up to it, there isn't any reason for you to stop having sex. Intimacy is very important in a relationship and just because you are pregnant is no reason to stop."

"Ok, thank you. Mason, do you have any questions?"

"Is there anything that would alert us something is wrong?

"Well, yes, cramping and any vaginal bleeding would warrant a phone call to me and possibly a trip to the hospital."

"Any other questions?"

"No, I don't think so," Angel says, looking at the doctor.

"Angel, go ahead and get dressed and I'll gather some information for you both," the doctor said. "Schedule another appointment with me in a month and if you have any questions, please call me. I'll leave the information for you at the front desk along with my business card."

"Ok, thank you," Angle says as the doctor closes the door behind her.

I help Angel up; she stands behind the curtain to get dressed. I sit back down and run my hands through my hair. I think I'm taking it better than I thought. I have sworn off alcohol from now on. The night I first proposed to Angel and she told me she was pregnant, I totally screwed that up. I got drunk and left her to deal with everything. That will never happen again. I am glad that I swore off cussing — especially out loud — when Angel was in the hospital. I need to be a better person for my family.

"Mason?"

"Yeah, um, I'm sorry, yes?"

"I asked you if you are ready to go. Are you all right? You seem like you're in deep thought."

I smile and stand. "You look stunning."

"Mmm, what got into you?"

"I'm just speaking the truth. Do you have everything?"

"The truth, huh? Let's go, Handsome. My head is spinning in circles from our visit today. A baby."

I hold the door open for Angel and place my hand in the small of her back, as she walks out into the hallway. "We sure got a lot of news in a short time."

"You can say that again," she laughs.

We check out and pick up the information at the front desk. I hold the car door open for Angel and wait for her to buckle up. I get in, start the car and sit there. I look over at Angel and smile.

"Well, I have to get to work. But when I get home tonight, we'll have a lot to talk about."

"Ok, I have some running around to do, but I'll be back to get you at 5:00."

I start the car and pull out into traffic. "If you finish early, you can hang out in the office until I get done, if you want."

"I might just do that."

"Come in through the back and the office will be unlocked."

CHAPTER TWO: OH, BABY

Angel

I drop Mason off at work and go to the library first. I don't have a clue about babies. Before, I would crawl into my black hole and cry — that was the old me. The new me is going to fight and try to keep it together. I know Mason loves me and wants to be with me, but I also know that this is a lot for him. I need to be strong for me and for him. I get the books I think will be the most helpful and head to the checkout.

Next, I head to the pharmacy and get my prescription filled for the Prenatal Vitamins. I take one right away, with some water I have in Mason's car. I go home and call Aunt Maria and Uncle Raùl. I don't tell them anything about the pregnancy; I just want to talk to them.

I tell her I am gifting them the beach house and I hope that maybe, one day, they will move down here. She tries to talk me out of gifting it to them, but the beach house belonged to my Aunt Rosie, Uncle Raùl's sister, so it should go back to them, and rightfully so.

I call Lilly next, to see if she, Bruce, and Madison could come to dinner tomorrow. I just want to be around family. I also call an attorney to set up a time with him to assist me with re-gifting the cottage.

On my way to Mason's office, I stop by Babies R Us. I just want to see what's in there. I walk in and I grab a cart. I walk up and down all the aisles and just look. The store is filled with everything, not just everything, but ten different kinds of the same thing in different sizes and colors. I stop by the baby clothing section and look at a preemie dress. All the clothing is so small. Can someone really fit in these? Now I understand why Brea was freaking out. I make a small purchase and head to the paint store. They have my samples all ready when I get there. I put the sample pallets for the Interior Design Business in the trunk of the car and head over to pick up Mason.

I text him to tell him I am on my way; I don't want him to worry. When I pull up, Mason is locking up the office and waves goodbye to Carla and Cathy. He doesn't get in the passenger seat — I didn't think he would. He opens the driver's side door and I smile.

"Get in, I'll drive," I say.

"Beauty has jokes. That was a one-time deal, and I won't let that happen again."

"I like driving you around," I say, as I take his hand.

Mason keeps ahold of my hand and walks me to the passenger-side door and opens it for me.

"You won't let what happen again?"

"I won't get drunk and expect you to take care of me again."

"I like taking care of you," I say, standing on my tiptoes to kiss him.

Mason wraps his arm around me and lifts me up. "I love you," he says, before he kisses me.

I kiss him back and then I tell him that I love him, too.

He smiles and lowers me to the ground. I probably shouldn't keep doing that.

I laugh. "Soon, I'll be too fat and you won't be able to lift me," I say, getting into the passenger seat.

Mason laughs and says, "Buckle up," and closes my door.

I buckle up and he gets into the driver seat and fastens his own seat belt. He looks into the back seat. "Did you do some shopping today?"

"A little. I made some decisions today and went ahead and put them into action."

"Really?" he asks, as he pulls out of the parking lot.

"I called your Mom and invited her, your Dad, and Madison to dinner tomorrow."

"Good, I haven't seen them much lately. Dinner will be nice."

"I also called Aunt Maria today and I told her I was gifting them the beach house. I called and made an appointment with an attorney today to draw up the paperwork. I want to gift them the beach house as soon as possible."

"You had a very productive day today." Mason looks over at me and smiles. "My Dad may be able to help you with gifting the beach house."

"Surprisingly, the news today didn't send me back to the black depression I used to live in. I do believe I owe that to you." I reach over and take his hand in mine.

"Beauty, I believe this is all you. You have always had inner strength; you just didn't know it."

"I don't know about that, but thank you. Do you think your Dad would mind helping with the legal paperwork for the cottage?"

"No, I think he would love to help."

We pull up into the garage at the beach house and Mason helps me out and then starts to reach for the items in the back seat.

"I'll get these, if you'll get the paint samples from the trunk," I say, reaching into the back seat.

"Ok, what are you planning on painting?"

I grab the bags from the back seat and close the car door behind me. "Nothing. Well, not yet anyway. It's for my Interior Designing Business. It's time I get it up and running, don't you think?"

"Have you decided on where you are going to set up your office?"

I follow him into the house. "I thought I would take your advice and work from home. I like it here and it's very motivating."

Mason closes the doors and locks up behind us. "I think that is a wonderful idea. I also think I give wonderful advice. Do you want to dine out for dinner tonight?"

"Sure, that sounds great."

"Ok, let me shower first, then I'll be ready."

Mason and I go out for pizza and salads for dinner. We talk about the news we received today at the doctor's office and about planning our wedding. He asks if I want to move the date up for the wedding, and I don't. I still don't want to interfere with Brea and Vincent's wedding. I ask him if the news we received today has changed any feelings he has, and it hasn't. He still feels this baby is his and he will love it, no matter what. I believe him; I have no reason not to. That eases a lot of stress from me. I would understand if it is too much for him. We did the pregnancy test, but I think we were still hoping it was wrong.

When we get home, we walk through the spare bedrooms and decide which will make the best room for my office.

We don't talk about the baby's room or a nursery or anything pertaining to children.

I have already spoken to Sara and Brea about leaving and told them that my last day will be Friday. It is bittersweet. I love them and love working for them, but this will be the ideal move for me, Mason, and our family. It's time I put my college degree to use.

The next day we clean the house and go to the grocery store. Mason's Mom, Dad, and sister are coming to dinner. I want everything to be perfect. We stop and get some fresh-cut flowers for the table before heading home.

I was going to cook, but Mason thought it would be too much, so he is going to have steaks on the grill. While the steaks marinate, we make potato salad, baked beans, and fruit salad. Mason is wearing his signature white linen shirt and a pair of plaid shorts. His hair is curly and unruly, and he smells of spice and sandalwood. The music is on the surround sound, and he is singing to every song that comes on. I love seeing him so carefree and happy.

I shower and dress in a white sundress to match Mason's white shirt. He sees me and walks over to me and lifts me up so we are eye to eye.

He smiles and says, "You look beautiful."

I wrap my arms around his neck. "Thank you, you look pretty handsome yourself."

The doorbell rings and Mason walks to the door still carrying me. I giggle, wrap my legs around his waist, and hold on so I won't fall. He opens the door wide for his family to enter, without putting me down and I laugh.

"Hi, come on in," I say, still laughing.

Mason slowly lowers me, and his Mom and Dad kiss and hug me before kissing and hugging Mason. Madison hugs me then Mason. I close the door and everyone gathers outside near the bar. Bruce pours Mason and himself a Scotch and pours champagne for Madison, Lilly, and me. I look over at Mason and notice that he is watching me. I don't say anything; I just take the champagne and smile. I have a bottle of water and I continue to drink it. Mason hasn't drunk any alcohol since my birthday. I wonder if he'll drink the Scotch.

He puts the steaks on the grill and walks over to me. "Are you feeling all right?"

"Yes, I'm fine. I didn't know what to say when Bruce handed me the champagne."

"It must have been a little awkward."

"It's fine, I just told them the heat was getting to me so I was going to stick to my water."

"Good thinking."

I kiss Mason before he returns to the grill to remove the steaks. Madison, Lilly, and I place all the food out on the large round outside table. Mason and I sit side by side, then Lilly, Bruce, and Madison seat themselves around the table. As always, the conversation flows easily as we talk about our recent engagement.

"Angel, I would love to throw you and Mason an engagement party and have some of our family and friends and Bruce's and Mason's colleagues come," Lilly says, with a gleam in her eyes.

"Lilly, that is very thoughtful and sweet of you, but Mason and I would rather not."

"Mom, Angel and I just want to keep this small, between our families," Mason says while squeezing my hand.

"I understand, but may I post the engagement in the newspaper? Something announcing the engagement with a photo of you both?" Lilly sits up straighter from across from the table and smiles. "Mason, I'm your mother and you'll get married only once. Please let me do to this for you, for you both."

Mason promises to provide his mother with a picture of us before they leave tonight. We ask her and Bruce about having the wedding in their backyard on New Year's Eve. They are excited about us getting married there and readily agree to open their home to us and our friends for the wedding. Lilly starts to cry and Bruce comforts her. Mason squeezes my hand under the table. Mason and I inform his mother that we want a small intimate wedding. She readily agrees.

Mason and Bruce clear the table, while Lilly, Madison, and I get the coffee and dessert ready. We sit at the table and talk about me quitting my job and starting my own business. We also talk about Mason selling his condo fully furnished and that he needs to go over tomorrow to clear out his personal belongings. Madison announces that she thinks the condo will sell quickly. She says that she often gets request for condos in that building and because it is the penthouse with the view it has, it will bring in several different buyers.

"Mason, I'll meet you at the condo tomorrow and we can get most of your personal items in a few trips," Bruce says.

"Can you go to the cottage and get my white desk and a few other items from there?"

"Oh, you're getting rid of the cottage?" Lilly asks.

"Well no, I'm gifting it to my aunt and uncle. It originally belonged to my Aunt Rosie, Raùl's sister. I am meeting with an attorney next week to help draw up the paperwork."

"Angel, save your money. I can assist you with that," Bruce offers.

"Thank you, I'll call and cancel my appointment on Monday. "

Mason tells his Mom and Dad that we would like to go to church with them Sunday. His mother is so excited and tells us Mason hasn't been to church in months. She tells us to be there at 11:00 a.m. sharp. After everyone leaves, Mason jumps in the shower and I pull out the items I bought from Babies R Us yesterday. I hold the small booties in my hand and smile. They are so tiny. I bought a pink pair and a blue pair. I tuck them away in my dresser and then take a quick shower.

Mason

I get out of the shower and walk into the bedroom, expecting to see Angel. I hear water in the bathroom so I know she is in the shower. I don't want to run into her wearing a towel or less. I dress quickly and head out to the lanai to make sure everything is cleaned up

The news we got at the doctor's yesterday was good news. The fetus is healthy as far as can be determined. Anything that is a part of Angel, I swear, I will love as much as I love her. She is amazing and beautiful. She doesn't have a clue how her beauty affects people. They stop what they are doing just to watch her. She has inner beauty to match her outer beauty, as well. She would give up her lunch to feed someone in need. I once saw her give a homeless man a sack lunch she had made for herself to eat. We watched him give half of the lunch to another homeless man.

Angel's inner strength is starting to show. I knew she had it; I just haven't seen it until now. She is coming to terms with being pregnant. I was afraid she would become depressed and shut herself out from the world and from me, but she didn't. It must still be hard on her to have a reminder of that night with Jim. I am so proud of her. I noticed she got some pregnancy books from the library, but hasn't opened them yet.

Angel walks out on the lanai wearing the white linen shirt I had on earlier. I look over at her and smile.

"Nice shirt."

She smiles, "It smells like you. I hope you don't mind my wearing it."

"What's mine is yours. If you promise to wear them all the time, I'll buy a dozen of them for you."

She walks over to me and reaches up to kiss me. "I love you."

"I love you, more," I say, kissing her back. "Do you want to take a walk on the beach?"

"Sure, I'll have to go change first."

"Come on, it's dark. There won't be anyone out here." I take her hand and we walk down to the beach. It's a full moon and the stars are out. The breeze blows Angel's hair away from her face and she looks stunning. Her long dark curly hair against my white shirt on her flawless body is gorgeous. She is so beautiful.

"What are you thinking about?" she asks, looking at me with a smile on her lips.

"I was thinking about how beautiful you look."

"Mason, I swear, you need glasses."

"You are always beautiful and you never know it. You have no idea how many people just stop and stare at you when you enter a room."

"Mason, that's not true and stop trying to embarrass me."

"See what I mean?"

Angel and I walk a short distance down the beach in silence and I notice her shiver.

"Come on, Beauty, let's head home." I take her hand and lead us in the direction of our beach house. "What are your plans tomorrow when Dad and I go to the condo?"

"I thought I would go to the cottage and pack up some of my things. I meet with your Dad next week to gift the cottage to Uncle Raùl and Aunt Maria."

I look over at her as she intertwines our fingers.

She says, "When my Aunt Rosie gave me the cottage, it was fully furnished. A few things in there belonged to my Mom, so I want those things. I also want the china cabinet with the serving dishes in it. I'll need to call Aunt Maria to make sure it's all right. That is, if you don't care? The furniture there won't really go well with your furniture."

"I'm sure they would want you to have whatever you want out of there. Don't worry about it matching or not. If you want it, we'll make it work. "

"I bet you didn't realize how little I was bringing into our relationship?"

"All I want is you; nothing else matters. What is mine is yours."

We walk the sandy path leading to the beach house, and I watch her walk up the stairs to the lanai. I want to look away, but I can't. My white shirt only goes mid-thigh and reveals her long tan legs. I can see the outline of her naked breast beneath the shirt. I adjust myself and walk up the stairs and lock the door behind us. I go right to the kitchen so Angel can't see the effect she has on me. The stronger and more independent she becomes, the more I want her. She was so broken when I met her. I just wanted to wait for her to heal and become the woman I knew was hiding beneath her tortured soul. Now that she is right where I knew she could be, I just want to make love to her and show her what it feels like to be loved. I don't think I have ever made real love to a woman before, but when it comes to Angel, I don't think it will be tough to figure it out. I used to crave it hard and fast, but with Angel I'm going to want it to last.

"Mason, what is wrong with you tonight? You are in such deep thought."

I look up from behind the refrigerator door that I am hiding behind and smile. "Nothing, I was getting us a water. That's all."

"No, you have been standing there for five minutes, looking at the picture of us on the refrigerator."

"I like that picture of us and I didn't realize you were timing me." I smile, close the refrigerator door, and open a bottle of water for her.

"Mmm, mmm. Come on, Handsome, let's go to bed. We have church in the morning."

I wake up to Angel crying. She is in bed and the lights are off. I blink a few times, trying to decide if she is having a nightmare, or if she is awake. Angel hasn't had a nightmare in a while. Lying near the edge of the bed, she cries softly. Angel usually sleeps right next to me or in the crook of my arm. Too much space is between us.

I scoot over to her and place my hand on her shoulder, "Angel," I say softly.

She continues to cry. I stroke her arm softly, again. "Angel, what's wrong?" Still no answer.

I think she may be asleep. I get out of bed and walk over to her side. She is lying in a fetal position on the bed and crying into the sheet. I kneel down beside her so I am eye to eye with her. I don't want to be towering over her when she wakes up; she still startles easily. I stroke my hand lightly along her cheek. She wakes up and looks at me. She doesn't startle like I thought she would. She blinks a few times.

"Are you all right, Angel?"

"It's my stomach."

"Your belly hurts?"

"It's cramping."

"Do you know for how long it's been hurting?"

"No."

"Have you been to the restroom?"

"No, I'm scared."

"Come on, Beauty, we need to see if you're bleeding. I'll help you." I pull the sheet back and help her up. She stands on shaky legs before walking into the bathroom. I wait by the door for her to come out. When she finally opens the door and walks out, she says, "No blood."

She takes my arm and walking with me to the bed.

I pull the covers back for her to get in. Do you know where your doctor's business card is?"

"No, but I have her number programed in my phone."

"Good girl." I walk over and get my medical bag from the closet and take her vital signs and check her pain level again. She says the cramping is better, but I'm not sure I believe her. Her blood pressure is elevated, indicating pain.

"Stay right here and lie on your side. I'm going to call the doctor."

Angel does exactly as I say, and I walk into the other room to make the call. I don't want to alarm her if I don't have to.

Once the conversation is over with her doctor, I take a bottle of water and some Tylenol into the bedroom with me for Angel. She is fast asleep. The doctor said for Angel to lie on her side and drink plenty of water and to take Tylenol for pain. She said if Angel begins to bleed to call her and take her to the hospital. She also said if she begins to miscarry, there isn't any way to stop it. We can only try to prevent it. I wake up Angel and give her the Tylenol and a drink of water. I tell her the doctor said to rest and she doesn't question me. I shut off the lights and climb in bed with her.

She is lying on her left side and has her back to me. I scoot close to her and kiss her head.

"Sweet dreams, Beauty. I love you."

"Good night, Mason. I love you, too."

Angel hasn't said much about the pregnancy since her doctor's appointment. I'm not sure what she is thinking. I know it will be hard on both of us if she carries to term. We will have a remembrance of Jim in our lives every single day. We'll get past it, but it will take time. It will also be hard if she miscarries. We both have had thoughts that we will feel guilty for having.

Angel reaches behind her, and I take her hand in mine. We often hold hands in bed. It's the closest non-intimate way to be with her. Sometimes I think I'm turning into a girl.

"Mason?"

"Angel?" I say, scooting even closer to her.

"Do you think God will punish me for saying I didn't think I could love this baby? Do you think he'll take it from me for saying hateful things?"

I stand up and walk over to the edge of the bed and kneel down beside her. I look her in her teary eyes and stroke her cheek.

"Beauty, I think God has a plan, I think God already had a plan and things will end up exactly as they should. Your thoughts are normal and should be expected. I don't think it matters what we say or do. Things will end up exactly as God has intended. If you deliver, you and I will be the parents of a beautiful baby and we will love him or her, with all that we are."

"What if I lose it?" She sniffles.

"Then we will mourn our loss and figure out the best way to move on. We'll spend time getting to know each other and planning our wedding. We'll talk about when the right time will be for us to start a family."

"You want kids with me?"

"Beauty, I want to fill this house up with kids who look just like you. I want to hear giggles and cries and laughter when I get home from work. I want to clean up spilled milk and change dirty diapers. Beauty, I want all those things with you and only you."

"I have a boy's name picked out, already."

"Mmm, should I be worried?"

"Nope, you'll love it."

"Well, since we are being honest, I have a girl's name picked out, too," I say, stroking her hair. "What's your name, then I'll tell you mine."

"Don't laugh."

"Ok."

"It's Alexson Bruce Myles."

I smile because I don't want to laugh. Alexson Bruce Myles. I get the Bruce name, but how did you come up with Alexson?"

"It's Mason Alexander combined, Alexson."

"That's your boy's name, huh?"

"Yup, your turn."

"Well, don't *you* laugh."

"Ok."

"My girl's name is Ana Maria."

She smiles to try to hide her laugh. "After the island? I like it," she giggles.

"No laughing."

"Mason, you can't name our daughter after Anna Maria Island."

"No, I can't. But, I can name our daughter after your mother, Ana, and after your Aunt Maria. Ana Maria Hope Myles."

Angel gets tears in her eyes and they fall down her cheek. Her lip begins to quiver. I wipe her tears away with my thumbs and lean in to kiss her quivering lips.

"Do you have any idea how much I love you?" I ask, kissing her again.

She kisses me back and nods. I can feel the warmth from her tears on my cheek. I pull away from her and look at her.

"I love you more than you'll ever know, and I thank God for bringing you into my life," she says, backing up and lifting the cover to me.

I get into the bed, pull her into my arms, and kiss her head. "Sweet dreams, Beauty," is all I say because I can't say anything else. I am definitely turning into a girl.

Angel

I wake up to cramping. I try not to worry; I know I can't change fate. Whatever God's plan is, no matter how I feel, I can't change God's plan. I have to believe things will be the way they were meant to be. I look at Mason; he is sound asleep. Funny that I can picture us together with a family. I didn't even know I wanted a family until I didn't have a choice. Mason wants to name our daughter after two women in my family. That speaks volumes about him. I have never loved anyone as much as I love him. He is so unbelievably amazing.

I cramp again and moan. Mason wakes up and looks startled.

"You're in pain." It's not a question but a direct statement.

"It's getting worse."

"Are you bleeding?"

"I don't think so. I haven't been to the restroom yet."

Mason sits up and looks at the clock. He hands me two more Tylenol and some more water. I drink the water and swallow the pills down.

"I have to pee."

I stand up and Mason is already out of bed. He walks me to the restroom and waits for me outside the door. I notice light pink blood on the toilet paper. I run water and get a panty liner from under the sink. I wash my hands and face then open the bathroom door.

"No blood," I lie.

There isn't anything he can do, so I'm not going to worry him. He takes my hand and walks me back into the bedroom and lifts the covers for me to climb under. I was thinking about staying up, but obviously Mason wants me to stay in bed. So, I do what he wants. I don't even question him.

"I need to call Mom and let her know we won't be going to church today."

"You should go. I'll be fine here."

The phone rings and Mason answers it immediately. He doesn't leave the room and I can hear what he is saying. It must be the doctor on the other end. I am surprised the doctor would call to check on me on a Sunday. I listen as I lie there. Mason looks over at me and then looks outside. He doesn't hand me the phone or ask me any questions. He hangs up the phone and looks over at me.

"That was your doctor calling to check in. She said she wants to see you in her office on Monday."

"Ok, I have work, so it'll have to be after that or during my lunch."

"Ok, we can go at lunch. She also said to stay in bed and rest today and if you start bleeding or cramping a lot to call her. Drink plenty of water and continue to lie on your side."

Mason climbs in bed with me to let me know that we are going to do exactly as the doctor wants. He picks up the phone and texts someone without saying a word. When he is done, he places the phone on the nightstand.

"Not going to church?"

"No, my girl needs me."

"Mason, you should go to church. We could use the prayers."

"Beauty, God hears our prayers no matter where we are. Being in church doesn't mean God will listen first or most or hardest."

"I guess you're right, but you don't need to stay here with me. It's just some mild cramping, it's nothing."

Mason stands without saying a word. He opens the blinds and walks out of the room. I lie there looking out into the private beach while lying on my left side. It is such a beautiful day with the sun shining. Mason comes back into the bedroom with a cup of coffee, a cranberry juice, two English muffins, and two bananas on a tray.

I sit up in bed and smile. "If you plan on staying in bed with me all day today, it's going to be very boring, you know."

Mason lays the tray across my lap, careful not to spill the coffee. He reaches down and grabs my computer and lays it at the foot of the bed, before he gets back into the bed.

"I thought we could shop, watch movies, eat, and sleep," he says while lifting the coffee from the tray.

I pick up the juice and take a drink. "That sounds like fun; what do you want to shop for?"

"I thought we could shop for office supplies for you: paint, fabrics, textiles, or whatever it is you'll need. You'll be needing samples and stuff. I assume you'll be meeting clients here, so you'll need an office to represent your work."

I hand Mason his English muffin and smile. "Yes, I guess, you're right. I already have the paint samples, but I'll need the fabrics and textiles, too. I'll also need to get some drapes, rugs, and lighting in that room I chose for my office. I don't think I put enough thought in this. I still have a lot to do before I'll be ready to start working."

"We have time, there isn't any hurry."

"I'll be out of work soon, so I am in a bit of a hurry," I say, finishing my juice.

"Beauty, you worry too much," he says and winks at me.

My cramping comes and goes throughout the day and the bleeding increases. It's not alarming so I don't say anything. Just as Mason has promised, we stay in bed and eat, sleep, watch movies, and shop. We bought lamps and rugs and ordered some textiles and fabric samples, all online. He called his sister and Dad and told them he isn't able to go to the condo to move his things today. His sister was more upset than I expected. She said she wanted to get it listed as soon as she could. Mason told her to list it right away and start showing it next week. The showings will be delayed by only a few days. In the meantime he'll be moving his things out. Mason makes soup and sandwiches for lunch and we eat in bed. He tells me it's nice staying in bed all day with me and doing nothing. Mason would never let me feel like I am a burden or he would rather be someplace else doing anything else. I have no idea what will happen with this pregnancy, but I do know that I am going to do everything I can to make him happy. I am so in love with him; all I want to do is marry him and be his.

After dinner and another movie, I doze off to sleep. I wake up to severe cramping. I feel wetness between my legs. I already know without looking. I yell for Mason because he isn't in bed with me. It is only a matter of seconds before he is by my side. I lie in a fetal position unable to acknowledge him in the room. He kneels down beside me.

"Beauty, are you cramping?"

"I'm bleeding." I can barely say the words through the pain.

Mason lifts the covers without saying anything. He lowers the covers and asks, "How bad is your pain?"

I can't say anything. I just rock back and forth. "We have to go to the hospital — just give me one minute." He doesn't wait for me to answer him before he walks away.

Mason makes a phone call, walks into the bathroom, and then digs into my dresser. He walks over to me and removes the covers. I am suddenly chilled. I keep my eyes closed, thinking it somehow helps with the pain.

"Angel, we need to get you cleaned up and to the hospital. Can you walk to the bathroom?"

I shake my head and ball into a fetal position even more. The pain is excruciating. Mason wraps his arms under my legs and back and lifts me up while saying, "Hold on."

He carries me into the bathroom and removes my blood-soaked panties. I sit on the toilet and he hands me a soapy washcloth. I bend over to wipe the wetness from my body and I am in shock at the amount of blood. Mason throws the washcloth in a trash bag, along with my panties, and hands me another soapy washcloth. Once I am cleaned up, he helps me get dressed and carries me to my SUV. He already has a towel on the seat and fastens my seat belt over me. He makes a phone call and tells someone we are on our way.

"Don't tell anyone."

"I won't, it was your doctor."

"Ok, are we almost there?" I grimace.

"Right around the corner, just a few more minutes. Hang on, Beauty."

Mason's phone rings and he answers it quickly. He says only a few words before hanging up.

"The hospital is expecting you. We won't have to wait in the reception area. Your doctor is also there waiting on you. She was already there seeing another patient when I called her."

"Oh, God, I think I'm bleeding through," I say, trying to gather the towel beneath me to thicken it.

We pull up at the hospital and Mason doesn't park. He pulls up along the curb near the E.R. entrance. Hospital staff are already waiting with a gurney and a wheelchair. I close my eyes tightly to try to ease the pain. Mason tells me to hang on and then I hear the car door close. He picks me up and lays me on the gurney. They tell Mason he needs to park the car and that he can't leave it there blocking the entrance. I hear Mason mumble something before I am taken inside. The doctor quickly examines me and Mason is by my side. He holds my hand and whispers in my ear how much he loves me.

Mason

I sit beside Angel in the recovery room. She lost the baby and has just had a D&C — dilation and curettage — done. It's a simple procedure where they go in and clean out her cervix. They remove anything that wasn't expelled through the miscarriage. I hold Angel's hand as she sleeps; I stroke her knuckles but she doesn't move.

I haven't cried or mourned the loss. I know it was God's will. I also know the baby would have been a reminder of Jim's attack. I would have loved that baby no matter what, but I also know that night would always be in the back of my head. I will never admit that or say it aloud. I am only human, and my feelings of hatred for Jim go very deep. I would do anything in my power to protect Angel.

She moans in her sleep and I stroke her hair and cheek. I used to do that to calm her, but I think I do it now because touching her calms me. It scares me, the effect this girl has on me. I would do anything for her. I sit beside her and just look at her. She didn't want me to call anyone today. She is such a private person. Everything she does she wants only a few people around. Only the few family members and the few friends she has will be at our wedding. Our wedding will have only about a dozen people there. Small and intimate, as she says. What she doesn't know is I am going to give her the wedding of her dreams. It will be small, but it will also be amazing. I plan on marrying only once in my life, and it will be to Angel. I am planning on going all out with the wedding and a honeymoon to match. She deserves to be treated like a princess. I haven't asked Brea to help, but I did ask Sara to help me. Brea is busy with her own wedding and preparing for the birth of their baby.

Angel moves and when I look at her, she is already awake.

"Hi."

"Hi," she croaks.

I offer her a sip of water and she takes it.

"Small sips," I say, and she nods.

"Did I lose the baby?"

"I'm sorry, Angel," I say, kissing her hand.

"Can I go home?"

"I don't know if you can go home tonight or tomorrow. Your doctor will be in very soon."

"I want to go home."

I lean in and kiss her. "I'll ask her when she comes in."

"No, tell her I'm going home. I don't want to be here all night."

At that time the doctor walks in. "I heard that, Angel."

We all smile at the doctor's comment. Angel looks a little embarrassed.

"I'm sorry. I didn't mean to be rude, but I want to go home."

"Let me check you out first, then we'll talk about sending you home."

I stroke Angel's knuckles before I stand to let her know it's all right. The doctor checks her chart, her vital signs, and

Angel's pain level, and then she shines a flashlight in her eyes and in her mouth.

"What are your plans for the next couple days?"

Angel clears her throat and says, "I have work and I have some books to return to the library."

Angel looks over at me and I shake my head.

"I mean, I'm going to stay home and rest."

The doctor looks over at me and smiles. "Mason, your girlfriend has spunk."

"Oh, you have no idea," I say.

I look over at Angel and she has her eyes closed. I know by now that the pain meds always make her groggy. "If I give you my word that she'll take it easy for the next few days, can I take her home? Angel has had a rough time the last few months."

"I understand that. I think she'll be fine to go home tonight. Bed rest for one day and she has to take it easy for 72 hours. "What kind of work does she do?"

"She an agent for an insurance company."

"She'll be fine returning to work on Tuesday. She'll still have some cramping and bleeding, but nothing as severe as she had today. I'll write her a script for pain meds to get her through the next few days."

"Ok, sounds great."

"Just give me a few minutes to get her discharge papers written up. I'll have my nurse come in and remove her IV and help her to get dressed."

"Thank you."

The nurse comes in and removes Angel's IV. They allow Angel to wear her hospital gown home since her other clothes have blood on them. She is still groggy but not as bad as I have seen her in the past. I get her discharge papers and sign for her to be released. Angel tries to listen to the doctor's instructions but falls asleep. She wakes up and listens again. I will help her remember the instructions, and I know she will follow them without any problems. Angel is the perfect patient. She always wants to do what is right.

We go home and Angel and I walk into the bedroom. She opens the top drawer of her dresser and removes two pairs of baby booties. She hold them and strokes them gingerly.

"I see you found the baby socks."

"These baby booties? I got them last week at Babies R Us. I guess we won't be needing them."

"You bought those?" Mason asks as he opens his top drawer to reveal two identical pairs. "I bought these shortly after you told me about the pregnancy."

Angel and I place the baby socks on her dresser side by side before going to bed.

The week flies by. Angel stays in bed on Monday while I work and I return her books to the library on the way home. I don't think she needs to be reminded of the miscarriage, even though I know she can't think of anything else. I called Angel off work with flu-like symptoms on Monday. Sara and Brea didn't question it. I called Josephine to come over and stay with Angel for the day. Angel wasn't happy about it, but she didn't argue with me either.

I take her to work and pick her up afterwards the rest of the week; it's a good routine that works for us. We order take-out for dinner most of the week to keep an easy routine at home. We didn't tell anyone about the miscarriage; Angel wanted to keep it private. Friday was Angel's official last day at the insurance company and they had a small going-away party for her. Angel has offered to help out while Brea has the baby and gets married and for other emergencies. Angel trained her replacement, Emma, this week so Monday should be a smooth transition for everyone. The samples came in the mail along with the lamps and rug she ordered, and this weekend I am packing up the condo and the cottage, while Angel decorates her office. She already has a client to meet with next week, so she needs to have her office ready. Dad drew up the papers for Angel to gift the cottage to her aunt and uncle. They received the papers in the mail yesterday and called to thank Angel for such a generous gift. They also told her to take whatever she wanted from the cottage. Angel wants only the spare bedroom furniture that belonged to her mother when she was a child, the shabby-chic china cabinet in the dining room that belonged to her Aunt Rosie, and the shabby-chic desk I gave her when we were broken up. Angel and I went over yesterday to pack up the china in the cabinet. She walked through the cottage picking up pictures and quilts before laying them back down. I know how much her family means to her and she'll miss this place. I hired someone to come in and clean the cottage once we get what she wants out of there. There is still food even I'm afraid to touch in the refrigerator. We don't mention or talk about the miscarriage. Madison has appointments to show the condo and she is on my butt to get my clothes out of the condo in a timely manner. I never should have said anything to her until I was already moved out. Too late now.

Dad backs the truck up to the garage doors and we get out. The truck is loaded with my things and things from Angel's cottage. This is our second trip *and* the last load. Madison will be happy now she can get the penthouse on the market.

The garage is filling up quickly. I didn't take anything from the condo except my personal things and some paintings Mom made for me. I did take a few extra things from the cottage for Angel. She wrote me a detailed list of the things she wanted but I added to the list. I brought some framed pictures and two other quilts that were there. The cottage doesn't have any regular blankets; they are all handmade quilts made by Angel's grandmother, mother, and aunts.

Angel walks out to the garage with a smile on her face. "Wow, is this the last load?"

"Thankfully it is," Dad says, getting out of the truck.

"I have a spot already picked out in the dining room for the china cabinet," Angel says while taking a box from the back seat. Dad looks over at me and smiles. "Do you want to rest before you unload it?"

"A water would be nice, first." I walk to the garage refrigerator and remove two bottles of cold water, and hand my Dad one.

Angel carries a few boxes into the house and holds the door open for my Dad and me. "Be careful with that," she says, directing us into the house. "I don't want you to nick it," she says, seriously.

Dad and I carry the desk and chair into the house before he leaves. Angel hugs him and thanks him for all of his hard work. She reminds him to save us a seat at church tomorrow. Dad tells us it's potluck after church so be sure to come hungry.

Angel is polishing the china cabinet and placing her china and serving dishes in it when I walk past her, carrying a large box. "What is that?"

"Just a few things on your list," I lie, and walk past her to her office. I lay the unopened box on the floor.

"That looks good in here," I say honestly, looking at the shabby-chic china cabinet.

Angel stands up and steps back to look at it. "Do you really think so?"

"I do. I like it." I look over at her and she is smiling while looking at the cabinet. "Thinking of a memory?"

"I am, how do you know?" She smiles, looking over at me.

"From the smile on your face. Care to share it with me?"

She turns to look at me. "I remember when Aunt Rosie bought this. We were at a flea market with my Momma and Dad. Aunt Rosie fell in love with it. My Dad hated it because he knew he was the one who was going to have to move it. He was the only man in the house, and he always had to do the heavy lifting and painting." Angel wipes a tear from her cheek. "Every summer Aunt Rosie would have a big project that needed done or something heavy that needed moved. Momma would bribe him with a sopapilla, a Mexican dessert."

"Bribing a man with food — she was a smart woman," I say, laughing.

"She was; my Dad loved Momma's cooking. Every day Momma and Aunt Rosie would cook and set the most beautiful table with these dishes. He would stuff himself full and then he would have to take a nap afterwards. He loved Momma so much. He fell apart when she died." Angel sniffles, and I take her in my arms and kiss the top of her head. I leave my lips there and kiss her again.

"I'm sorry. If she was anything like you, I know how much he must have loved her."

She pulls back and looks at me with tears in her eyes. "Mason, that is the sweetest thing you have ever said to me, thank you."

"It's true, I can imagine his grief when she passed from this life to the next one. I pray I never have to go through it. I would be lost without you."

"I love you."

"Beauty, I will always love you more," I say, kissing her.

The next morning, one week post miscarriage, Angel and I go to church together. She made some soup and bread for the potluck and some sopapillas for dessert. Before church I ate some of what she made — the house smelled wonderful and I couldn't resist.

We walk into church and Mom and Dad are waiting for us inside the door. Dad and I take the food into the kitchen while Mom and Angel find a seat.

After church Mom walks Angel around the room and introduces her to everyone. I forgot how much I enjoy church. Everyone is so nice and polite. We sit and eat together and talk about our wedding. Mom has a notebook and jots down some of Angel's ideas and what she would like. Angel reminds her that we want something small. Nothing fancy, just small and intimate. Mom nods and continues to write. Angel wants white twinkling lights, candles, and white daisies as the flowers for the wedding. Nothing else seems to matter.

"Mason, what colors do you think we should go with? It'll be winter and New Year's Eve."

"Beauty, whatever you want; as long as you are walking down the aisle, nothing else matters."

"I was thinking black, white, and gold. What do you think?"

"I think it's perfect."

Mom smiles and writes that down, too. I'll need to get with Angel later to see what she really wants. "We haven't talked about the wedding party. Do you know how many you want to attend?" I ask.

"Oh, I guess we haven't talked about that. I don't really have that many friends or family here. Most of the guests will be your friends and family."

I take her hand and hold it in both of mine. "We'll keep it small."

We talk some more about the wedding and about having dinner together next week. Angel says she'll try to get her aunt to come down from L.A. and help with the wedding details.

On the drive home, Angel asks if we can stop by Carl and Josephine's house. But before we do, she wants to stop by the store first. Angel shops for non-perishable items. She is cautious in choosing what she buys. We walk through the garden section and she sees an angel holding a baby and places it in the cart. I don't say anything. I just continue to push the cart in the direction she walks.

We arrive at Carl and Josephine's unannounced. She removes the angel holding the baby and lays it on the seat before she takes any of the bags out of the car. I take the remaining bags and follow her to the front porch.

We stay and visit for a while. Angel tells them about the engagement and about the upcoming wedding. She tells them about their new neighbors, Maria and Raùl, and hopes they move into it one day soon. We say our goodbyes and shop for our own groceries before heading home.

Once we are home, we put away the groceries and Angel tells me she's going into her office to put the rest of her things away. She seems quiet tonight, and I am not sure why. I give her some time before I go and check on her. The door is slightly open, and I can hear her crying. I look in and see her sitting on the floor holding the angel she bought earlier. I walk in and sit on the floor beside her. I hold my arms out for her and she leans into them.

"What's wrong, Beauty?" I say, rocking her back and forth.

"I'm sad."

"About the baby?"

"No, yes. I mean no, but I am. It sounds stupid, I know. I listened closely to the service today at church talking about life and death and how it's important to live your life to the fullest and to love and appreciate everything, no matter how small. It got me thinking about things."

I pick her up so she is on my lap. She laughs. "Beauty, you do that. You are so grateful for everything you have and treat people with so much respect. I think you live your life to the fullest every day."

"Mason," she says, looking at the porcelain angel she is holding. "I was pregnant with a baby I didn't know I wanted. It will never have a chance to live. It was here and now it's gone, forever. I was so cruel to think I may never be able to love it." She cries. "What kind of beast does that? Thinks that?"

"Angel, you have been through so much. You have been through so much in just the short time I have known you. The truth be told, I didn't know I wanted to be a Dad until you were pregnant. I thought I would be happy living my life with just me in it. Your pregnancy and the picture I had in my head of us as a family, made me realize I want a family with you."

"Really?"

"I was also scared that the baby would remind me of that night Jim attacked you and I was afraid of that. I didn't want to be reminded of that night and I didn't want to look at an innocent newborn baby and have those feelings."

"Mason, I didn't know that. I am so sorry."

"My point is, it wasn't just you feeling that way — it was me, too." I look at her and twirl a piece of her hair with my fingers. "I think it's normal to feel that, but I also think that if you had carried to term, we would love our baby no matter what. I think the thoughts we had would have been replaced with the love a mother and father have for their child."

"I love you," she says.

"I love you, more."

Angel

Later that night, Mason walks outside with me and watches me place the porcelain angel and baby in the flower garden. He tells me we all need an angel to look after us. We lie in bed and talk about the wedding and I take notes. Mason says that he would like Vincent and Donovan in the wedding and adds that he would like to have them both as his best man. I tell him it's our wedding and if he can't choose which one to ask then he should ask them both. I also tell him I would like Madison, Sara, and Brea in the wedding. I tell him I need to ask Uncle Raùl to walk me down the aisle.

Mason asks where I would like to honeymoon and I don't have a clue. I have been only to Puerto Rico and that was a very long time ago. I have family there but haven't seen them in a very long time. We decide on black, white, and gold as the colors for the wedding, and we will start looking at wedding cakes soon. We don't need a venue since it's at his parents' house, so that's good.

I wake up before Mason and make him breakfast before he goes to work. I shower and dress first, although I have no place I need to be today. I should be heading into work, but I no longer work there as of Friday. I'll run into town and pick up some more samples and get ready to meet my first client, Marilyn, on Wednesday. I'm a little nervous. She wants her lanai redecorated for a luau she is planning. It's not a small lanai — it's the size of Mason's beach house. I'm excited and if it goes well, I'm hoping she'll use me for other rooms in her house.

Mason walks into the kitchen already showered and wearing his scrubs. Although he has his own practice and could wear a suit or dress pants, he chooses to wear scrubs. Today he is wearing a Spiderman scrub top.

"Hi, what are you wearing?"

"No jokes, please. Mrs. Green is bringing in her twin sons for a physical today for sports."

"No jokes, I was just thinking how sexy you are wearing Spiderman scrubs." I walk over to him and wrap my arms around his neck. "You do know how hot that is, right?"

"Um, no. You like Spiderman?"

"No, but I like it when you wear Spiderman. I didn't know it, but you look so very, very sexy in those," I say, kissing him after every word.

"Mmm," he moans kissing me back. He lifts me up and walks us, still kissing, towards the kitchen table. "I like it when you think I'm sexy," he says, putting me down beside my chair.

Mason pulls my chair out for me and pushes it in slightly when I am seated.

"Let's eat, Beauty, you're starting to embarrass me."

We talk about helping Brea and Vincent move into their new house. We all are going over tonight to see it. They still have landscaping they are working on, but the inside is completely finished. Their baby is due in four weeks, and their wedding is in seven weeks. It's hard to believe she is that far along.

Mason leaves for work, and I leave right behind him. I have some things I need to pick up for Brea and Vincent's baby. I want to have some things in the house for their son when they visit. I am also hoping we can keep him overnight some time. I run my errands, have lunch with Bruce's mom, Lilly, and have dinner made when Mason gets home. We eat and go to Vincent and Brea's new home. Vincent has asked me to decorate the nursery as a surprise to Brea before they move in. He gave me the room measurements and told me after I see the room to let him know what else I need.

We drive to their newly built, unfurnished home. Mason enters the code at the gate and then drives down the winding paved driveway. The large two-story pale yellow with white trim home comes into view. A very pregnant Brea is sitting on a rocking chair, and Vincent, Sara, and Donovan are gathered near her on the wrap-around porch.

Mason and I walk hand in hand up the stairs and are greeted warmly. Brea doesn't stand, but she smiles. I walk over to her and hug her. She looks more tired than usual. Vincent helps her up and we walk into the house.

We enter through the large double doors; the home is open and spacious. White walls, hardwood floors, vaulted ceilings, and large bay windows are throughout the house. To the right is a large grand wooden staircase, and to the left is a large office, den, or library — I'm not sure what they'll use it as.

We walk through the open living room; the kitchen is on the left with a bar, an island, and a breakfast nook. A large formal dining room is on the right side of the breakfast nook. To the right of the living room is a bedroom, a conjoined bathroom, and another bedroom. We walk up the stairs while Brea stays downstairs sitting on the only chair in the house. The white walls, hardwood floors, and vaulted ceilings continue up to the second floor. The master suite has a large bathroom with his and her sinks, a shower, and a separate bathtub. It also has two large walk-in closets and another smaller room. This would normally be a seating area, but Vincent said that he wants this room to be the nursery. He said if he didn't have the nursery nearby, Brea would never be in their room.

I take out my notebook and draw a diagram of the room. I note where the windows, closet, and door placements are. I walk through the rest of the house with Mason, Sara, and Donovan, while Vincent goes downstairs to be with Brea. Two more bedrooms and another bath are on the upstairs floor. After Mason and I walk through the other rooms, we walk back into the master bedroom and Sara and Donovan go back downstairs to join Brea and Vincent.

I walk around the empty nursery and open the closet. Inside, a few tiny outfits are hanging up. I pick one up and touch it lightly. Mason comes up behind me and kisses the top of my head. I lean into him and close my eyes.

"I love you," I whisper.

He kisses the top of my head again and says, "I love you, more."

I hang the outfit back up and turn to hug Mason.

He asks, "Are you ready to go downstairs with the others?"

"I am."

"Do you have everything you need?"

I tuck the notebook back into my purse. "I do. Lead the way, Handsome."

I follow Mason down the stairs; Brea is still sitting down. I walk over to her and kneel down beside her. "Are you all right?" I ask.

"I'm fine, just tired. It's these Braxton Hicks contractions. They aren't real contractions; however, they feel like they are real. They keep coming and getting stronger."

"How long have you been having them?" Mason interrupts.

"Off and on for a few months," Brea laughs.

Mason laughs, too. "Today, Brea. How long have you had them, today?"

"Since I got off work."

"Angel, would you go to the car and get my medical bag, please?" Mason says, kneeling down beside Brea.

I walk out to the car and wonder how many medical bags he has. When I walk back into the house, Vincent has stress lines on his face. I hand Mason the medical bag and step away so he can assess Brea.

I stand beside Sara and she immediately grabs my hand.

"She doesn't look good," Sara whispers.

"I know, how was she at work today?"

"She seemed fine, a little bitchy, but that's normal for her. She had her feet propped up on a chair most of the day because of the swelling to her ankles."

"Is swelling normal?" I ask.

"How the hell do I know?"

We both laugh at her comment. Mason stands up and tells Vincent to take Brea home to rest. He tells him it is just Braxton Hicks contractions, and he doesn't need to worry.

"Brea, drink plenty of water and keep your feet elevated. You still have four more weeks before Junior is born."

"Mason, stop calling him Junior. He has a name."

"Oh, I didn't realize you decided on a name. What is it?"

"I don't know yet, but I know it isn't Junior." Brea says, trying to get up from the chair. "I also know it isn't Dweezil or Kal-El."

"What, you don't want to name your son after Frank Zappa's son or Nicolas Cage's son?" Mason smiles. "Nic Cage is a big Superman fan, and Kal-El is the name of Superman's father. And did you know that Penn Gillette of Penn and Teller fame named his daughter Moxie Crimefather? He said that he likes the name Moxie because it is so American, but the name Crimefighter is a joke. When his daughter grows up and begins to drive and is pulled over for speeding, he wants her to be able to say, 'But, officer, we're on the same side! My middle name is Crimefighter!'"

We all laugh but Vincent. I know Brea has been moody lately, and I imagine it isn't any fun for him. I tell Brea to call me if she wants me to cover for her at work tomorrow.

Vincent helps Brea down the stairs while Donovan locks up the house. Vincent has his truck and Brea moans as she tries to climb into the truck.

"Here, take our car and we'll take the truck," I offer. "It'll be easier for Brea to get in and out of," I say.

"Are you sure?" Vincent asks.

"Vincent, just help me in the car, will you?" Brea says, holding her belly.

Mason smiles as Vincent walks Brea over to the passenger-side door. I hold it open for them, and Brea gets in and fastens her seat belt. Vincent stands and Mason smiles at him. Vincent doesn't smile back, but he takes the keys from Mason and thanks him. I hug Brea and tell her I'll see her later and to call me if she needs me.

We watch them drive off and talk to Donovan and Sara for a while.

"Is she in labor?" Sara asks.

"No, she isn't. She's having something called Braxton Hicks contractions."

"You mean she's bitchy like that during a fake contraction? Poor Vincent." Sara laughs.

"Come on, Sara, let's go home. You're going to have a big day tomorrow if Brea shows up for work," Donovan says, walking over to his truck and holding the door open for her.

Sara and I hug and Mason holds the truck door open for me, too. On the way home, I ask Mason if he wants to stop by the Babies R Us store for a few minutes.

"Sure, it's on the way. Is there something special you're looking for?"

"I have the measurements for the nursery and Vincent gave me his credit card. I thought we could walk in and see what they have in stock. Judging from the way Brea looks, I'm not sure how much longer she'll hold out. She's due in four weeks."

Mason reaches over and holds my hand and smiles at me as he pulls into the Babies R Us parking lot.

"Why are you looking at me like that?"

"I can't look at my girl and smile?" he says, putting the car into park.

"Not when I don't know why you're smiling."

He lets go of my hand and laughs. "Beauty, stay put." That is all he says before getting out of the truck and walking over to my side to open the door.

Mason

Still smiling, I open the truck door for Angel. She reaches her hand out for mine and slides out of the tall truck. We walk into the large store and I take a cart. Angel walks behind me and takes another cart for her.

"Planning on spending all Vincent's money?" I laugh.

"I'm planning on spending most of his and some of yours." Angel also laughs as she walks away from me. I follow her up and down the aisles. She looks at bedding, curtains, and rugs and after deciding on the perfect ones, she places them in *my* cart and smiles. She looks at baby car seats and asks me which the best one for a newborn is. We discuss the different kinds, types, and brands before she places one in *her* cart.

Is there anything else you want to look at?" I ask.

"Just a few more things."

I follow Angel down the baby-clothes aisle. She picks up a few blankets, sleepers, a couple of bottles, a bag of diapers, and some baby socks and puts them in *her* cart. I pick up a sleeper with a sailboat on it and a pair of baby socks and put them in *my* cart. Angel smiles when I look up.

"Here, let me have them; this cart belongs to *us*."

I hand her the sleeper and booties and ask, "All of that is ours?" I look into her cart, which is filled with the baby car seat and diapers.

"Yes, I want *Junior* to stay the night sometime."

We both laugh at her calling the baby Junior. "I wouldn't call him that in front of Brea, if I were you."

"I know — she was a little short tempered when you called her son Junior."

We pay for our purchase, load up the truck, and head home.

Once everything is unloaded in the house, Angel does a load of laundry. She washes all of the new baby items and begins to open the box with the car seat in it.

"Beauty, wait for me and I'll do that. I just need a quick shower."

"Ok," she says, not looking at me and still trying to open the large box.

I shake my head and smile as I walk over to her. Angel is fighting with the box to pull the car seat out of it. I laugh and she looks up at me; her hair is loose from her ponytail, and her hair is falling around her face.

"I thought you were going to shower?"

"I was, but it looks like I need to rescue you from this."

"How do they get all this in here?" she asks as she tries to pull the large car seat from the box.

"Here, Beauty. Let me help you before you hurt yourself."

The next day, I get a text from Vincent saying Brea is feeling better and will be going to work. Angel has a meeting with one of her clients. She is scared, although she has nothing to be afraid of. I called yesterday to have a bouquet of daisies delivered to her. After work tonight, she wants to go over to Brea and Vincent's new home and set up the nursery. Vincent said he would have all the baby furniture in the room when we get there.

The week goes by with painting Vincent and Brea's nursery on Wednesday, and hanging curtains and moving everything into the nursery on Thursday. Brea went to the doctor and has already started to dilate. Vincent has hired a moving company to move their things into the new house next weekend. He said he is excited to get moved before the baby arrives. Brea's Mom is flying in the week after. Angel has been over to her new client's house trying to figure out the best décor for the lanai. She has been doing some online shopping for specialty pieces for her client and helping out at the insurance company when she can. Angel and I have an appointment on Monday with Cakes and Cups to decide on our wedding cake. Madison said she has a buyer for the condo and the price is being negotiated. She adds that I know her. I almost choke when she tells me the buyer is Julia. I don't care who buys it as long as it sells. I do wonder why she would be interested in the penthouse.

I sit outside on the lanai drinking a Scotch waiting on Angel. I'm taking her to dinner tonight. We have a wonderful relationship, and I can't wait to marry her. I'm wearing a midnight black suit with a white shirt and a gray tie. I know she likes that Grey guy in the books, so I thought I would humor her. I stand when I hear Angel.

She is standing at the doorway holding a glass of white wine. I look her up and down like it's the first time I saw her. Her hair is down and straight, and she has full red lips. She is wearing gold hoop earrings, a red form-fitting dress that shows off her cleavage, and black heels with a red bow on each back. My eyes slowly travel up her gorgeous body. I smile when our eyes finally meet.

She smiles and says, "See something you like, Handsome?" Angel turns around slowly so I can see her front and back. She stands tall and with confidence.

"Nice shoes," I say, as I walk over to her grinning. "You look absolutely stunning." I bend down slightly to kiss her. When she wears five- or six-inch heels, she is almost as tall as I am. I haven't seen this outfit on her in a very long time.

"Thank you. You remember this dress?"

"I will never forget *that* dress. You wore it the first night you spilled your drink all over me at the club."

"Um, you mean the night you spilled your own drink on you." She laughs.

"I remember it differently, but it's the same night."

She wraps her arms around me. I inhale her scent. Peaches and cinnamon. My favorite scent.

"Umm, did you just sniff my hair?" She laughs.

"No," I lie. "That would be a little creepy," I say, backing away from her so I don't sniff her again.

Angel laughs because she already knows the truth. I love the way she smells and I love inhaling her scent. It's better than any drug out there and it calms me instantly.

"You look very handsome tonight, and a little *Fifty Shades of Grey*, I might add."

I smile, adjust my tie, and straighten my cuffs on my shirt. "I do? I didn't realize."

"You didn't realize that gray tie, or any gray tie for that matter, doesn't remind me or any other women out there, of Christian Grey?"

I straighten my tie again and give her my all dimpled smile, "How am I supposed to know gray ties remind women of that *Grey guy*?" I lie again. I took her *Fifty Shades of Grey* book to the office with me a few weeks ago. I read it during my lunch breaks because I wanted to see what the hype is. Any man, if he is smart, should read that book. When they say a man could learn a thing or two from that book, they aren't kidding. Angel and I still haven't made love, and if she turns out to be a freak, I wanna be ready.

"What are you smiling about?" Angel laughs.

She brings me from my thoughts. I'm not about to tell her what I was thinking. "Come on, Beauty. We have reservations we need to keep."

Once we arrive at the restaurant, we are led to a small intimate table for two. I had some daisies and baby's-breath delivered — they are in a bud vase decorating the center of the table. The server sees us and walks over to help Angel with her chair. I give him a dirty look and he backs away. *She's mine, Dickhead,* I think to myself. Angel looks over her shoulder at me and smiles. She knows the jealous beast inside me wants to come out. I push her chair in slightly before taking the seat across from her.

"The flowers are beautiful," she says, picking them up to smell them. "Odd that our table is the only table with daisies."

I look around the room at the other tables. "Yes, it is."

"Mason, I know you ordered these specifically for me. Thank you."

"You're welcome. I want something on our table as unique as the woman I am with."

"Did I tell you I love you today?"

"You did, but you can tell me again."

"I love you, Handsome."

"I'll always love you more, Beauty."

I smile at her and look around the room. Julia walks into the restaurant with someone, a girl. I look away and square my shoulders before looking back to Angel.

"What's wrong?"

"Nothing," I lie.

The waiter returns with our menus and tells us the specials. Angel orders a glass of white wine and I order myself a Scotch. Julia unfortunately is seated not far from us.

The waiter leaves and I reach over and take Angel's hand in mine. I square my shoulders and roll my neck side to side.

"What's wrong?"

I smile at her. "Nothing."

Angel doesn't pick up her menu but turns around in her chair and looks around the room. My strong girl knows I am on edge and wants to protect me. I squeeze her hand and she turns back around.

"This restaurant will let just about anyone in here." Angel says, smiling and squeezing my hand back.

The waiter comes over with our drinks.

I raise my glass to hers, "A toast."

She smiles, and raises her glass to mine. "To new beginnings?"

"To new beginnings," I repeat, and clink my glass to hers.

She lays her menu over to the edge of the table without even looking at it. I look over the entrees and decide quickly. I always order for her and I always order two of the same meal. I figure if we eat the same thing at home, we might as well eat the same thing while we are out together. Fortunately, we have the same taste in food.

The waiter comes over and smiles at Angel and asks, "Have you decided?"

I clear my throat, so he knows to look at me, not her. "We'll both start off with the Tenderloin Carpaccio, New Zealand petite lamb chops, red-skinned potatoes, and spinach salads. That'll be all," I say, dismissing him. Angel look at me and smiles.

He nods and turns to walk away without looking over at Angel.

"Mason?"

"Angel?" I say, looking into her big brown eyes. "I don't like the way these dickheads look at you." I already know what she is going to say.

"Would you rather they come to the table and ignore me, treating me as if I don't exist?" she says, with a raised brow.

"No, of course not. I would rather have a waitress. They don't look at you like they want to have you for dinner." I lean forward in my chair.

"No, you're right, they don't, because they are too busy looking at you like they are going to eat you for dessert."

"Well, lucky for you, I don't like dessert."

We both laugh when we realize how silly we sound.

The waiter returns with our appetizers. Angel places her white linen napkin on her lap. I watch from the corner of my eye as Julia stands and stumbles in our direction. I know we aren't near the restrooms, because I always request a table as far away from them as I can get. When she gets closer to our table, I stand, buttoning up my jacket.

"Julia," I say, taking a step to be closer to Angel. I place my hand on the back of her chair to keep some distance between them.

"Well, if it isn't the happily engaged couple," Julia slurs.

I feel Angel's chair slide back slightly as she stands up. "Julia." Angel smiles.

I reach over and take Angel's hand in mine. "I take it you saw the announcement in the Sunday paper."

"Who didn't? Your engagement picture and announcement took up the entire page."

Angel smiles at me and loops her arm around mine. "Thank you. Yes, my future mother-in-law is pretty excited about the upcoming wedding. We wanted something small to announce our engagement." Angel stands a little taller and winks at me. Oh, my girl wants to play. I can do that.

"Yes, Mom did get a bit carried away with the announcement." I smile.

"Angel, you know, I have no idea what Jim ever saw in you." Julia slurs her words and stumbles. "Angel, how does it feel to know you are responsible for a man's death?" I can feel Angel tense up and shiver. I caress her arm with my hand and stand in front of her.

I step closer and whisper to Julia, "Get the fuck out."

I think, *Sometimes — but rarely — the f-word is the absolute best word to use.*

"What, Mason, the truth hurts?" Julia stumbles again.

At that time her friend walks over to us. "Jules, let's go," she says, taking Julia by the arm.

"Julia, I swear, if you don't leave now, I will get you disbarred. I will show evidence that you are stalking and harassing Angel. You leave now and don't you ever speak to Angel again."

"You can't do that. That would be a lie."

"Are you so certain? Do you want to try me? It seems to me like you are stalking and harassing her," I say, taking another step closer to her. "I swear, I won't stop until you lose everything."

"Is everything all right?"

I look up — the manager of the restaurant is standing nearby.

"Everything's fine. These lovely ladies are just leaving and please see that I get their check." I smile. "They may also need a ride home, if you can arrange that for them as well?"

"Certainly sir, it's my pleasure. Ladies, this way," he says, holding his hand out towards the front of the restaurant. I reach behind me and Angel takes my hand. They begin to walk away and I say, "Julia, should I assume our business here is finished?"

Julia turns around and looks at me with glassy eyes, "Yes, Mason."

"Very good. Ladies, you both have a lovely evening."

Angel

Mason turns around and hugs me. I wrap my arms around him and cuddle into him. I inhale his spice and sandalwood scent. He always smells so good. I hear someone walk up to us and Mason shakes his head.

"Please box this up for us; we'll take it to go."

I pull away from Mason's embrace and look towards the waiter. "No, that's all right; we'll be staying."

"Angel?"

I look up at Mason and smile. "I'm fine, I need to use the powder room first. I'll be right back."

Mason nods to the waiter and walks me to the powder room.

"Let me guess, you'll be right here waiting on me?" I smile.

"You may want to hurry unless you like cold lamb chops." He also smiles.

I walk into the empty powder room and look at my reflection in the mirror. Surprisingly, I have held it together. No crying, no red eyes. I wash my hands, straighten my dress, and stand tall. I walk out of the powder room and Mason is facing me talking to the restaurant manager. I walk over to him and he never takes his eyes off me. He abruptly ends his conversation with the manager.

"Are you sure you want to stay?" he asks, his eyes searching mine for the truth.

"I am here with the most handsome man in the world and a delicious meal waiting for us. I am not about to let Julia ruin our evening," I say, honestly.

"That's my girl." Mason places his hand on the small of my back and leads us to our table. As always, he holds my chair out for me and pushes it in slightly once I am seated. He sits across from me and smiles.

We both place the white linen napkin on our laps. "Most handsome man in the world, huh?" Mason, says smugly. He picks up our untouched, now cold appetizers and sets them on the edge of the table.

I look up from my food to look at him. He is watching me, smiling. Even after the scene with Julia, he still smiles. No stress lines, just a beautiful dimpled smile. I love him and can't wait to marry him. "Yes, I would say you're the most handsome man in the world, and I can't wait to marry you."

"Oh, Beauty, I plan on spending every day of my life making you happy." He reaches over and takes my hand in his. He fingers my engagement ring and looks at me with dark eyes. "I would marry you today."

Neither of us has touched our food. I hear footsteps behind me and Mason waves whoever it is off.

"Angel, I wanted to talk to you about something, and this seems like a good time."

He lays his fork down and leans in a little closer to the table. He is still holding my hand with one of his. I look at him and can see the seriousness in his eyes. I lean forward so he knows that he has my undivided attention.

"I want you to hear me out, before saying anything, all right?"

"All right."

He sits up taller in his chair and gives me a lop-sided smile. "I can't wait to marry you and I can't wait to have a family with you. If you would agree, I would marry you right here, right now." He looks around the dining room and then back at me. "I didn't know I wanted a child or a family, until it was taken from me." He fingers my engagement ring again, and, never taking his eyes off mine, says, "I have thought long and hard about this and would like to start trying for a family with you, right away. As soon as we are married, I want to start. I know this seems fast and maybe you need time, but I want you and a houseful of little girls and boys who look just like you. I want to be surrounded by you or a part of you every day, as soon as I can."

My vision gets blurred from the tears and I can barely see. I stand, never letting go of his hand, and walk the short distance to Mason. He doesn't stand and pulls me onto his lap. He wraps his arms around my waist and I wrap my arms around his neck. "Mason, I love you more than the air I breathe. I want nothing more than a bunch of little boys and girls, with dark curly hair and big dimples." I kiss Mason with all the passion and love that I have for him.

"Is that a yes?" He smiles, pulling back to look at me.

"Yes, that is definitely a yes."

Mason reaches up to wipe the tears from my cheek. "You know, I am the happiest man in the room right now, right?"

We both look around the room and it is empty. "Happiest man in the room, huh." We look over at our waiter, and we both laugh. The waiter does not look happy. "Well, that was pretty easy, since the only other man in the room is pissed because we are still here."

"We need to start eating earlier," Mason says, waving to the waiter.

"Or leaving earlier." We laugh.

The waiter boxes up our food and Mason pays our check along with Julia's check. He stands tall, buttons his jacket, walks over to me, and pulls my chair from the table for me to stand. He reaches his hand out for me and I take it. *I will always take his outreached hand.* Mason grazes my arm with his fingers and I get goose bumps. "Cold?" he asks.

"Yes," I lie.

Mason's touch still gives me goose bumps, but I'm not about to share that secret with him.

CHAPTER THREE: TINY MIRACLES AND HUGE BLESSINGS

Mason

I hold Angel's car door open for her as the valet stands by. I know the valet usually does this, but there is something about someone helping Angel that bothers me. I want to be the one who does that for her. I want to be the one who does *everything* for her. I tip the valet and get into the car. Looking over at Angel, I am surprised to see her seat belt isn't on. "Buckle up, Beauty."

I fasten my seat belt and look over at her. "Um, Mason," she says, holding her cell phone on her lap. My phone dings, alerting me of an incoming text. "You may want to get that."

Not sure what is going on, I reach for my phone. It's a text from Vincent.

V: Heading to the hospital, Brea's water broke.

I look over at Angel with a grin. She has a twinkle in her eyes and the biggest smile I have ever seen. "Do you want to go to the hospital?"

"Can we?"

"Let's go home and change into something more comfortable, first." I text Vincent back:

M: Heading home to change first, then we'll be there. Hang in there.

V: Mom, Dad, Sara, and Donovan are on their way. Hurry, man, this shit is scary.

M: It'll be fine, be there in an hour.

"Let's hurry, I don't want to miss anything," she says, fastening her seat belt.

Once she is fastened in securely, I pull out into traffic. "Be prepared for a long night. First-time babies usually aren't in any hurry to leave their warm and comfortable home."

Angel and I change into jeans and tee shirts. I grab a couple hoodies from my closet for us. Angel disappears into the closet and returns carrying a gift, wrapped in pale blue foil paper with a white silk ribbon and bow. She tucks a card inside the ribbon.

"You bought the baby a gift?"

"Well, it's more for Vincent and Brea. Do you think it's stupid I did that? It's from the both of us. Maybe I should leave it here."

"Beauty, I think it's a wonderful idea that you did that. I wish I had thought of that."

"Well, that is why you have me." She smiles.

"One of the many reasons," I reply. "Do you have everything?"

She looks around the room. "Camera, I need a camera."

I smile as I hold it up for her to see.

"And that is why I have you," she laughs. "We are a perfect pair."

"That we are. Let's go, Beauty, and welcome our new nephew into the world."

We arrive at the hospital and make our way to the Labor and Delivery room waiting area. Vincent is there, looking disheveled. He is at the coffee pot pouring himself a cup. His Mom and Dad are already here. Angel and I walk over to his parents and his Mom and Dad stand up. I shake his Dad's hand and hug his Mom. "Angel, this is Vincent's Mom, Serena, and you remember his Dad, Vincenzo."

Angel takes a step closer and reaches her hand out for Vincenzo's.

Vincenzo ignores her hand and leans in to embrace her, saying, "Nonsense with the formalities, how are you?"

"Very well, thank you."

She steps back and looks over at Vincent's Mom.

"Oh, Mason, she is just as beautiful as you described." Serena leans in and hugs Angel.

They welcome her lovingly, just as I knew they would.

"Thank you," Angel whispers.

I know this show of affection is embarrassing to Angel.

"It's lovely to finally meet you," Angel says, backing away from her.

Vincent walks over and cups my shoulder with his hand. "Man, what took you so long?"

I look at my watch. I said we'll be here in an hour and it's been only 45 minutes. "Sorry, we got here as quickly as we could. How is she?"

"They're in there doing whatever they do. Something about an IV and some other shit. She's crying in pain and blaming me for causing it."

I look over at Angel and she raises a brow.

Vincent's Dad laughs. "I almost forgot about that. Son, you'll need to be careful holding her hand. You have no idea how strong a woman is until she is in pain."

Serena lightly touches her husband's arm. "Vincenzo, be nice."

"Yes, Dad, be nice. I'm already afraid to go back in there." We all laugh.

Sara and Donovan walk in and Sara is carrying a bouquet of Happy Birthday balloons. I look at Donovan and he shrugs his shoulders. *It must be a girl thing.*

"Well, look who decides to stroll in," Vincent glares at Donovan.

Donovan looks at the clock on the wall. "I said an hour. We're five minutes late."

Sara puts the balloons on the end table and walks over to Vincent and hugs him. "Having a tough time?"

"I'm sorry. It feels like it's been three days since I texted you guys."

"It's all right? How's our girl?"

"Bitchy, in pain, blaming me for causing it."

Sara laughs. "How long has she been like that?"

"For about four weeks now." We all laugh again.

"Well, you should be used to it by now."

Sara walks over to Vincent's Mom and Dad. Donovan walks over to Vincent, and I walk over to sit with Angel. We talk for a few minutes until the nurse comes in and says, "Vincent, you can go back."

He looks around the room, "I'm scared. I don't want to go in there yet."

Vincenzo laughs. "I don't blame you, son."

Serena stands. "Sara, Angel, and I will go in first." She looks over at her husband sternly, "Vincenzo, be nice."

Vincenzo smiles and holds his hands up, "All right, I'll be nice. Kiss Brea for me."

The girls all leave and head towards Brea's room.

"Did you call Brea's Mom?" I ask because I honestly have no idea what else to say.

"Brea called her as soon as her water broke. Brea's Mom, Dad, her three sisters and Sara's Mom are catching the next available flight."

I look at my watch; it is 11:01 pm. It's 8:01 am in California. I walk through the room with my cell phone trying to find a spot where I have service. I send a text to Maria and Raùl, just to let them know that Brea is in labor and we probably won't have phone service in case they need to reach Angel.

The girls return and tell us Brea has had an epidural and is resting comfortably.

"Is she asleep?" Vincent asks, nervously.

"Yes, Vincent, she is asleep; you can go in. The epidural numbs her from the waist down so she can't feel any real pain, just pressure."

"Oh, thank God." He stands to walk out the door.

"Vincent?" his mother says.

Vincent turns around to look at his mother. She stands and walks over to him. She places both of her hands on his cheeks and rubs her thumbs side to side. "Vincent, this is one day you will never forget. Enjoy it, no matter how bad it seems to get. This is a monumental moment in your life. In a few hours, your son, my grandson, will be born."

Angel takes my hand in hers and loops our fingers together. I look at her and see that she has tears in her eyes. I squeeze her hand to let her know I am here.

Vincent leans down and kisses his mother on each side of her cheeks. "What if I mess this up? What if I'm not ready to be a Dad?"

"Vincent?" she says, still cupping his cheeks. "Look at your father. Do you think for one minute that he would raise a son who isn't capable of being the best son, husband, and father that he can be?" She looks him in the eyes and I swear my eyes get misty.

"No, Mom. I know he raised me better than that."

"Then you go in there and give your support to Brea because she is counting on you. Just be there for her and let her know how much you love her."

Vincent swallows, and I know he is trying not to choke on his words. "Thank you, Mom. I'll be back with updates, when I can."

He walks out the door without looking back. We wait and talk about the upcoming birth. This is the first grandchild on both sides of the Salvatore and Kinsley family. Most of Vincent's family still live in Italy and with Vincent being an only child, this baby is already loved. Vincent told me that his mother has set up a nursery in his old bedroom for the baby.

"Mason and Donovan?" Vincenzo says.

We both look up at him.

"I hate to ask this, but it is the weekend. With the baby coming early, Brea and Vincent are living out of boxes in their old house. I was thinking we all could help out and get them moved into their new house."

"Say no more. I don't have any plans for this weekend," Donovan states.

"The movers aren't scheduled to move them for another week. You wouldn't mind giving up your weekend and helping me move them into their new home, would you?"

"Vincenzo, I can't think of a better way to spend my weekend," I say.

"I may be able to hire some of Vincent's employees to help out," he adds.

"When are you wanting to move them?" Donovan asks.

"As soon as the baby is born and we know everyone is healthy."

"Sounds like a plan."

"Angel and I will go over and help put things away," Sara says while looping her fingers in Donovan's.

"You would do that?" Vincenzo asks, looking at both girls.

Sara and Angel look at each other. "Of course, we would. We love Brea and Vincent. If you can use our help, we would love to contribute."

"Thank you. Brea and Vincent are very blessed to have such great friends," Serena says, softly.

Vincenzo gets on his phone and sends out a text to someone.

The door opens and Vincent walks through it. We all stand and stare at him.

"She's still resting; she is exhausted. Sara, have you heard from her Mom yet?"

"They are all at the airport in baggage claim. Maybe another hour or so. They were able to fly into Sarasota instead of Tampa."

"That's great. Mom and Dad, if you want to go see her, she was asking for you."

Vincenzo and Selena stand and leave the room. Vincent comes in and pours himself several cups of cold water from the water cooler. He looks exhausted. He leans up in the chair and rests his elbows on his knees.

"Is everything all right?" I say, sitting beside him. Donovan comes over and sits on the other side of him.

"Man, I don't know what to say. My head is spinning. There is so much scary shit going on in that room."

"What kind of scary stuff are you talking about?" I ask.

"She's hooked up to monitors that keep beeping, she's feeling pressure, nurses and doctors are in and out."

"All that sounds normal. I think she's in good hands. Are you sure that is all that's bothering you?"

Vincent runs his hands through his hair. "Dude, in a few hours I'm going to be a Dad. A Dad. I'm going to be a Dad. I'm scared that I'll mess that up. Look at me. What do I know about being a Dad?"

Donovan looks over at Sara for help. Sara and Angel walk over and Sara kneels down in front of Vincent.

"Vincent, you and Brea will make wonderful parents. The love you have for each other will help you with parenthood. It will come to you as soon as you hold your new son. Your son, Vincent. No one will care for that baby any better than you and Brea."

Vincent looks up at Sara and smiles. "I hope you're right. I am so afraid I will screw this up."

"You won't," she smiles.

Vincenzo and Selena walk back into the room. "She's asking for you, Vincent."

Vincent stands and walks to the door before stopping. He turns around and looks around the room. He looks at the Happy Birthday balloons and the blue-wrapped gift sitting on the end table. He smiles.

"Thank you all for coming to share in the birth of our son. It means a lot to us both. I hope you know we wouldn't be able to do it without your support."

He turns and walks out of the room before anyone can say anything.

Angel

The words Vincent just spoke brought tears to my eyes. Sara holds my hands. I look over at her — she has tears in her eyes. I have never seen him so unsure of himself. He is such a strong, powerful, and in-control man. How can he be afraid of messing fatherhood up?

I walk over to Selena and ask how Brea is doing. She looks up with teary eyes.

"Are you all right?"

"Yes, dear. I'm fine, thank you."

"Do you need some water or something?"

"Another tissue would be wonderful, thank you."

"I'll be right back."

I walk over to the coffee maker to get a box of tissues sitting next to it. Mason is standing there with Sara and Donovan.

"I wonder if Selena's all right?" I say, looking at Mason.

"I'm sure she's fine. I think it's the first-time emotions of being a grandparent. All of a sudden, this seems so real. In a few hours they'll be grandparents. She'll be fine."

"I hope you're right."

I walk back to Selena and hand her a few tissues. I lay the full box on the table beside her.

"May I sit?"

"Yes, please."

"Vincent tells me you decorated a nursery in your home for the baby."

Selena's eyes light up. "Oh, we did — it's just beautiful. I found the cutest bedding for little boys. Have you ever seen those cute little bugs they have now with the lime green background decorated on the bedding?"

"The ones at Babies R Us with the frogs, bees, and caterpillars? They have the matching curtains, rugs, and even a plush mobile for the bed?"

"Yes, that's the one. I did the room in those. Vincenzo painted the walls lime green and it is so cheerful and happy. We even found some plush stuffed animals to match."

I smile, partly because I had seen those and they were darling, but I also smile because I didn't choose those for Brea and Vincent's nursery. "I'm sure the baby will love it."

"Thank you, I am so excited, I can't wait to hold him and have him stay over."

At that time the door opens and in walks Sara's Mom and Brea's Mom, Dad, and sisters.

"Did we miss it?" Doris asks.

Vincent's Mom and Dad stand.

"No, we are still waiting," Selena says. "She's resting. They gave her an epidural to help with her pain."

"Oh, thank God," Doris says, placing her luggage in the far right corner. "I want to see her."

"I'll walk you out to the nurses' station." Selena and Doris walk out the door.

Vincenzo and John gather around the coffee maker while Sara and Brea's sisters head towards the restroom. Mason walks over to me and sits beside me.

"Are you hungry? You didn't eat dinner," he says, taking my hand in his.

"Neither one of us has eaten since lunch. I'm thirsty. I'm tired of water and coffee. I wish they had some juice."

Vincent walks into the room. He looks even more exhausted. He walks over and sits down beside Mason. Donovan walks over to the coffee maker, returns with a cup of coffee, and hands it to Vincent.

"Thanks, man. I wish I had something stronger."

"Sorry, it's all we have. How is she?"

"Sleeping in between contractions. She is exhausted."

"How much has she dilated?" Mason asks.

"Five, she dilated to five."

"Well she's halfway there, so that's good news. How are you feeling?"

"I just want to support her and be there for her, but I have no idea how. She cries that her back hurts so I rub her back, and then she yells that she's hot so I get her a cool washcloth, and then she yells that she's thirsty so I get her ice chips, and then she yells that she wants water. Man, I didn't know she was this bitchy. Will she always be like that?"

"No, Brea's a sweetheart. Her body is going through some changes and it's talking a toll on her. It won't be long, so hang in there."

Vincenzo comes over and kneels in front of Vincent. "You know, your grandfather Arturo once said that your grandmother was the sweetest woman he ever knew, except during childbirth. You have to remember that it's not easy on her. As soon as the baby is born, she will go right back to being that sweet and wonderful girl you fell in love with."

"I sure hope so."

The girls come back in the room followed by Brea's and Vincent's mothers. "She's asking for you, Vincent."

Vincent goes back to be with Brea.

"They have such strong family ties. I realize how much I miss my family."

I reach for my phone in my purse. "I'm going to look for a place in the hospital where I can have phone service. I want to call my Aunt Maria and tell her about Brea being in labor and tell her how much I love and miss her."

"Do you want me to walk with you?"

"No, stay here, I'll be right back. I love you."

"Beauty, I love you, more."

I walk the short distance down the hall to a large bay window with a small leather and wood loveseat that sits under it. I sit down and decide to send out a text. It's late and I don't need to wake them.

A: I'm sitting at the hospital waiting on the birth of Brea and Vincent's baby. I realize how important family is and how much I love and miss you and Uncle Raùl. I may not tell you often enough, but I do. Brea's family and Sara's Mom all flew in for the birth. Being surrounded by their family makes me happy and sad. I'm happy for them, but sad for me. I have so few family members here in the states and I never get to see them. I'm feeling sorry for myself. I'm sorry. The beach house is sitting empty, so anytime you're ready to visit, it's there. I love you both.

I hear a noise and look up to see Mason standing in front of me. I wipe the tears away from my cheek with the back of my hand; I didn't realize I was even crying. Mason doesn't say anything, but he sits beside me. He lifts me up and sets me on his lap. I bury my face in his neck and inhale deeply.

He leans back and looks at me, "Did you just sniff me?" He laughs.

I wipe my eyes and nose with the backs of my hands. "No, my nose is running," I lie.

I bury my face in his neck again and take another deep breath. He smells like his signature scent, spice and sandalwood. He smells like home, comfort, and love. This is a smell that will always comfort me. I swear, I could inhale him all day.

Mason rocks me and doesn't say anything. He kisses the top of my head and leaves his mouth there. He inhales deeply. We sit in the loveseat at the end of the hall in silence.

My phone chimes that I have a text. I look around and see that it is now daylight. I look at the clock on the wall: 8:14 a.m. I reach for my phone, realizing I had fallen asleep. I check my phone while still sitting on Mason's lap and it's from my Aunt Maria.

A.M.: Angel, I just saw that you texted. Your Uncle Raùl is still in bed. We both love and miss you more than you'll ever know. If we could, we would move down there now. I still have work and so does Raùl. I'll visit as soon as I can. Please, congratulate Brea and Vincent on the birth of their new baby. We love you, Pumpkin.

Mason's phone dings that he has an incoming text. He reads it.

"Mom, Dad, and Madison are here with breakfast. I'm going to get Donovan to help me carry everything up."

I stand up from Mason's lap and turn around to extend my hand to help him up. He laughs before reaching for it. He stands up and leans forward, then backward. He moves his head from side to side.

"I'm sorry. I didn't mean to fall asleep on you."

"I'm not," he laughs. "Let's find Donovan to help me." He takes my hand and we walk down the hall and into the Labor and Delivery waiting room. The waiting room is full of Brea's and Vincent's family and friends. The time is 8:28 a.m. Brea's sisters are all playing cards in the back of the room, Vincent's and Brea's parents are gathered at a sitting area on the right and Sara is sound asleep on Donovan's lap on a couch to the left of the room.

"I'm going to make fresh coffee while you wake sleeping beauty."

"Great idea. I almost hate to bother them," he says, walking over to the couch where they are asleep.

I empty the old coffee and start two fresh pots. I walk over to the only free table and remove the magazines and empty coffee cups from it. Sara comes over with some disinfecting wipes that she got from the counter top near the coffee pot and starts wiping the table down. Mason, Donovan, Bruce, Lilly, and Madison all walk in carrying two bags each, which are filled with drinks and glass casserole dishes of food, as well as other items. They look around the room and see Sara and me and walk over to us. They set everything on the table and then walk around the room exchanging pleasantries with everyone. Sara, Donovan, Mason, and I start to arrange the food and drinks on the table. I open the paper plates, napkins, cups, and plasticware and set them out. The casseroles smell delicious. Potatoes, ham, onion, egg, and cheese. I place the homemade biscuits near the casseroles and my mouth begins to water from the aroma. Mason walks over to me and hands me a cup of cranberry juice.

"Drink up."

I back away from the table so others can start filling their plates.

"Thank you, I'm so thirsty." I take the cup from him and down the juice in one gulp. He laughs.

"Let's eat, I'm starving," he says taking the empty glass from me.

Mason and I are the last to eat, and I am surprised to see how much food is left.

Mason and I get our food and sit in the corner of the room with his family. The door opens and in walks Donovan's parents. I sometimes forget that Vincent, Donovan, and Mason all grew up together. They walk over to hug Sara and Donovan before walking around the room and exchanging pleasantries with everyone else. Mason introduces Roger and Cam to me, although Roger and I have already met. He was at the celebration the night Vincent found out he was having a son. It was the night we came home from our trip to Ohio early.

I walk away and leave the families to talk. After I make a plate of food for Vincent, I wrap it up, and set it off to the side. Sara and Brea's sisters come over and help me clear the table. I look over at Mason and see that he is watching me. He always keeps such a close eye on me. I get goose bumps just thinking about him. I smile at him and continue the cleanup.

Sara walks over to me and whispers in my ear, "Get a room."

"Trust me, I would." We both laugh because we both know that isn't going to happen. I look over at Mason and he raises a brow at me. I look away because he is just so sexy. Vincent walks in with a smile. He looks around the room and says, "Mom and Doris, Brea wants you." I warm up his plate of food while Sara pours him a coffee and a juice. He announces to everyone that Brea has dilated to eight and the epidural has helped, before taking a seat at the table.

"How is she?" John asks.

"She's complaining of back pain, so I rubbed her back during her contraction and continued rubbing her back after her contraction ended. She then yelled at me to leave her alone. With Brea, I have learned that less is best."

Vincenzo, Bruce, John, and Roger all laugh. Everyone else just looks at them.

"My son is a smart man to figure this out on his own," Vincenzo says proudly.

Bruce adds, "I didn't figure that out until Lilly was in labor with Madison."

"Thanks for telling me, I appreciate that," Vincent says with a twinkle in his eyes.

"Some things a man needs to figure things out on his own." John laughs as he cups his hand on Vincent's shoulder.

Vincent finally eats. He downs his drink and eats quickly. I'm not sure if he is hungry or trying to hurry in case Brea is ready.

Doris walks in the room with a smile. "Vincent, it's time for Brea to start pushing."

Everyone starts to clap in excitement. Vincent walks to the door and turns around.

"What's the date?" he asks.

"It's September 13th," Johns says.

He looks at the clock; it is 10:14 a.m. "My son's birthday will be September 13th. The next time you see me, I'll be a dad."

Vincent looks pale and Mason walks over to him.

"Vincent, you'll be fine and you'll be a wonderful Dad. Now, go in there and help Brea with Junior," Mason says, laughing.

Vincent laughs, too. "You better not let Brea hear you call him that."

"Trust me, I won't make that mistake again."

Vincent looks around the room. Vincenzo walks up and hands Vincent his camera. "I don't care who, but have someone take pictures of my grandson."

Vincent takes the camera and nods before he exits the room with Doris.

Once they both leave the room, Sylvia says, "When I was in labor, I was having a lot of pain but I was not dilated far enough to push; they didn't have epidural back then for pain, and they wouldn't give me anything stronger for fear of it affecting the baby. The bitchy nurse I had, kept telling me to find my focal point and breath. I had no idea what the hell she was talking about and finally screamed at her, 'What the hell is a focal point?' She then said, 'It was obvious that you haven't taken the time to take Lamaze classes,' to which I responded, 'They didn't offer Lamaze during the midnight hours when I was available.' I was so grateful when she went off duty. Shortly after, a super-sweet nurse came on duty."

Cam added a story about one of her childbirths as well. "When I was in labor for Donovan, I was scared and didn't know what to expect. At one point when I was screaming and crying and the nurse said, 'Honey, you're going to scare the other moms if you keep screaming.' I yelled back, 'They SHOULD be scared!'"

Vincenzo laughs and holds up his right hand.

"Do you see this?" he says, pointing to his little finger.

We all nod at his crooked finger.

"Selena broke it when she was in labor with Vincent. I was holding her hand during a contraction and she squeezed so hard she snapped it."

We all laugh.

"As soon as Vincent was born, I had to go downstairs to the E.R. for an x-ray and they were able to set it," he says, flexing his hands. "It's almost good as new. People think I injured it at work; I just let them think that."

Mason gets a text and reads it quickly. "I have to pick something up from downstairs. I'll be right back."

"Hurry up, I don't want you to miss anything."

"I'll just be a few minutes."

Vincenzo and John start to pace the room. Brea's and Vincent's Moms are allowed in the room with Brea since they are the grandparents. Sara, Donovan, and Sara's mother, Sylvia, are on the couch. Brea's sisters are huddled together and Bruce, Lilly, Madison, and I wait near the front table. I pour myself a cup of juice and wish my self-pity would pass. I have Mason's family here, and these people in the room are my friends. I am so blessed, and yet here I am feeling sorry for myself.

I miss my family. I miss having a Mom to share my joy with. I blink back the tears that threaten to fall. It is such an emotional day.

The door opens and in walks Mason carrying two suitcases. He holds the door open wide and in walks Maria. I smile and look at Mason and then Maria and then back to Mason. I almost run over to her. I wrap her small body in my arms.

"I didn't know you were coming," I say, leaning back away from her to make sure it's her.

"I didn't know either — thank Mason for this. I had some time off work and Mason surprised me with a plane ticket. He wanted me to be here with you. Now that I am here, I know this is where I belong."

I look at Mason, "You did this?"

"It's nothing. I thought it would be nice to have some of your family here with you."

I hug Maria again and turn to Mason. I hug him and squeeze him tightly. "Thank you so much. I love you."

He drops the luggage and wraps both arms around me. "There isn't anything I wouldn't do for you. I love you."

I let go of Mason and lead Aunt Maria to the table. Mason sets the luggage in the corner of the room and walks over to us.

"Any news on Junior?"

Everyone laughs, "No news, Bruce says."

I look at the clock: 12:05 p.m. Almost an hour. How long does it take to push a human being through a hole the size of a nostril? *It could takes days*, I think to myself. *This baby could be born today, tomorrow, and the day after tomorrow. That is a joke — a joke I will not tell anyone.*

"How long are you staying?" I ask Aunt Maria.

She looks at Mason, "I took an early retirement so I'm here to stay. I'll have to fly back to see your uncle and he'll come here sometimes. Until your uncle retires in December, he and I will have a long-distance relationship. I will fly back once in a while to see him, and he will fly here once in a while to see me."

"You're staying? You'll be here for the wedding? Oh, my God, you can help me with the wedding!"

"Yes, Pumpkin, I wouldn't miss being here to share in your happiness. I wish I could have come sooner. I was going to surprise you next week, but Mason and Raùl thought I should come now. I see now that they were right."

Doris and Selena walk into the room with smiles plastered to their faces. We all stand.

"Brea and Vincent have a healthy baby boy. He was born at 11:44 a.m. weighing in at 7 lbs and 6 oz. and he is 22 inches long," Doris says, beaming.

John and Vincenzo bow their head as if praying.

The room cheers and everyone hugs each other. "The nurses said you can start going in, two or three at a time," Selena adds.

"This is great news," I say.

"Yes, Beauty, it certainly is. We have a baby boy in our circle."

"Would you mind if we say a prayer, to thank God for such a tiny miracle?" I ask.

Everyone stands and holds hands. I clear my throat, bow my head, and close my eyes.

"Dear Heavenly Father, We would like to take this time to thank you for watching over Brea while she brings a new precious life into this world. We would like to thank you for giving us the gift of a miracle. A new baby is the beginning of all things — wonder, hope, and a dream of possibilities. This baby is a true blessing, and we pray that you continue to watch over Brea, Vincent, and their child. In your name we pray, Amen."

"Amen."

Everyone decides who will go in first after the grandparents. I feel overwhelmed all of a sudden.

"Mason?"

"Beauty, what is it?"

"Where's the chapel? I feel like I need a few minutes with God."

"It's on the third floor. Are you all right?"

I smile at him so he can see I am more than fine. "I have been so blessed today, with Aunt Maria and our new little addition to our group. I need to thank God in private. I hope you can understand."

"Of course, I'll go with you if you want me to."

"No, stay here and wait in line so we can see them," I say, looking around the nearly packed room.

Mason

I wait with my family and Maria. The grandparents went back together, then Brea's sister will go next. We'll go in last to see them. Angel has been in the chapel for well over an hour. I think about going to look for her when she finally enters the room — her eyes are puffy and red. I walk over to her and ask, "Are you all right?"

"Better than ever. Just counting our tiny miracles and huge blessings."

I bend down and whisper in her ear, "You're my blessing," then I kiss the shell of her ear. "And I love you," I say, kissing her again.

"You guys can go in now."

We look up and see the nurse standing there holding the door open. I reach over and hand Angel her blue-wrapped gift and hand Sara the Happy Birthday balloons. We follow Sara and Donovan down the long hallway leading to Brea's room.

The door is shut. Sara quietly opens the door before looking back at us. She peeks in and then slowly opens the door further. I lift my camera and make sure the flash is off; I don't want to startle Junior. We walk in and I close the door behind us. Brea is asleep on the bed holding the baby and Vincent is right beside her, also sound asleep. I raise my camera and snap several pictures. They look so peaceful that I don't want to wake them. Vincent has his hands resting on the baby.

The nurse comes into the room and we move out of her way. Brea and Vincent wake up and smile at us. We wait until the nurse checks on Mom and the baby. Once the nurse leaves, we walk closer to the bed.

"Do you want to meet your new nephew?"

We all nod in unison.

Brea opens the blanket and reveals a beautiful baby boy. She removes his hat so we can see his full head of black hair. "Please meet Arturo Vincenzo Salvatore."

Brea and Vincent beam.

"He's beautiful," I say.

Brea says, "He is beautiful, but he has a big bump on his head. The doctor says that it is nothing to worry about. It will disappear soon."

Vincent says, "The doctor joked that it is an intelligence bump. He said that it's where the extra IQ points are stored until they can properly be distributed in Arturo's brain."

The girls lay their gifts down and scramble to the sink to wash their hands so they can hold the baby. Vincent kisses Brea and the baby before he stands. We shake his hand to congratulate him. I also hug Brea after Donovan and congratulate her. I look at the baby, but don't touch him. He looks like a beautiful British Prime Minister Winston Churchill, although it may not seem like such a thing is possible. If anyone wants to know what Arturo will look like at age eighty, they should look at him now. Most baby boys look like little old men, although sometimes they have more hair at birth than they will in old age. Arturo has pink skin, a perfect nose, mouth, and eyes. He also has the most hair I have ever seen on a baby. Brea looks at him and smiles, then she replaces his hat and covers him back up. Sara and Angel walk over to Brea and the baby. I turn so I have a better view of Angel. She hands Brea the blue-wrapped gift while Sara holds the baby. Brea smiles and unwraps the gift with excitement. Brea looks radiant. She doesn't look like the villain Vincent made her out to be earlier. Brea holds up the gold 8x10 picture frame. *Nice gift,* I think to myself. Angel looks at me and I nod and smile to let her know, it's perfect. I focus my attention back on Vincent.

"She pushed like only 20 minutes. She did so well; I am so proud of her."

That isn't what he was saying earlier. Donovan and I laugh.

"I love Brea more now than I ever thought possible. She gave me a child, our child."

I have to swallow the lump in my throat. *That is pretty special.*

"Arturo looks just like me, although I wished he looked like her."

I don't say that the baby looks like Winston Churchill.

"He is pretty amazing," Donovan says, watching Sara rock the baby side to side.

We talk about the baby and how well Brea did. Vincent talks about all the people who have been here and how wonderful it has been and how grateful he is that we all are here to share it with him. I look back over at Angel; she is holding the baby to her chest and she is rocking him side to side. I notice she doesn't look sad or unhappy about the recent loss of her baby. I see only joy and happiness on her face.

"You're a very lucky man, Vincent. You have it all," I say, honestly.

"Yes, I think so, too."

"It's my turn to hold the baby."

I walk over to the sink and scrub my hands. Donovan is right behind me. I walk over and hold my hands out for the baby. Angel smiles and gently hands him to me. I hold him up gently so I can see him. I am careful to support his head; we all are.

"Arturo Vincenzo Salvatore; it means strong."

"Yes, Mason," Brea says, 'Arturo' means 'strong as a bear.'"

I am a childhood friend of Vincent's and I know Arturo is a family name. It was Vincent's grandfather's name. I kiss the baby on the forehead.

"I like it, but I like Junior better."

Everyone laughs and I kiss the baby again. I hand the baby to Donovan, who holds him gingerly. The baby, young Arturo, begins to fuss.

"Brea, I think he's hungry."

"Ok, let's try this again." Brea sits up in bed and reaches for the baby.

This is the perfect time for us to leave. We say our goodbyes with hugs and kisses to the family.

We walk to the cafeteria, get a drink, and join the rest of the family at a table. Everyone decides to meet at Vincent and Brea's home in two hours to begin the moving process. We want to start moving them as soon as possible. I have no idea how long it will take. We get Maria's suitcase and take her to the beach house with us. I knew she was coming in, but I didn't think to get food in the house for her. She'll also need a car to drive. Poor planning on my part.

We go home, shower, eat, and head over to Vincent's house. I get a text to meet everyone at the new house. As we pull into the driveway, we see Vincent's foreman there and two large trucks backed up to the garage. We get out and head into the house. The house is full of boxes and furniture.

"This is the last of the stuff," Vincenzo smiles.

"Really?"

"I know. I'm a little shocked, too. Vincent's foreman and the other workers have been at it all day."

Angel and Maria walk around the house. I see people unloading boxes in the kitchen. Someone is in each of the bathrooms and I hear more people upstairs.

"Can you help with the rest of the stuff in the truck?"

"Sure." I walk out and start unloading the truck. It is mostly boxes and everything is labeled with what room it needs to go in. Once we have everything unloaded from the truck, Vincenzo walks the guys out. Everyone who was at the hospital is here. Everyone is here helping Brea and Vincent get moved into their new house before they bring the baby home. I smile.

"What are you smiling at, Handsome?" Angels asks as she wraps her arms around my waist.

I look down at her and smile. "Just the way everyone has come together to help. It is very heartwarming to know that people still do that."

"I know, can you believe that? Nobody had any rest after staying up and waiting for Arturo to be born, and look at them."

I follow Angel into another room and she starts telling the guys what to do and where to put things. She moves boxes out of the way and tells us to put the furniture where she wants it. I haven't seen Vincenzo in a while. When I finally see him, he is standing on a ladder hanging hardware for the curtains. I can't help but laugh.

He looks down at me. "That girl of yours is a pretty little thing, but she sure is bossy." He laughs.

"Mason, come and help me." I hear Angel call from the other room, and I laugh, too.

"Oh, you have no idea."

"I think I do, son. I sure didn't want to do this tonight, but I couldn't tell her no." He holds the electric screwdriver up and starts screwing a screw into the wall. *She does hold a lot of power.*

I walk into the dining room and Angel is struggling with an area rug. She has delegated work to everyone and this place is looking great. It was a disorganized mess when we got here. Once the rug is in place, we center the dining room table and chairs on it. Once she is satisfied, we walk upstairs and see Brea's sisters working on the master bedroom and bath. Sara, Sylvia, and Cam are in the closets hanging clothes and putting items on the shelves. Angel looks into a few boxes and pulls out clean bed linen.

"Go over there," she says, pointing to the other side of the bed.

"You are a bossy little thing." I laugh as I walk to the other side of the bed.

"Do you want to stand there, or do you want to get this done so we can go home?"

"Toss me a sheet."

"That's what I thought."

We make the bed and then go into the guest bathroom and start unloading boxes. I hang the shower curtain while Angel puts the towels and washcloths in the linen closet. Once we are done, she looks around and nods.

"Come on."

"Yes, ma'am." I follow her downstairs and we move some more furniture around. She leaves me and walks into the kitchen. She opens the refrigerator and talks to Doris and Selena for a minute. She opens more cabinets and says something else. A few minutes later Selena and Doris walk into the room and tell John and Vincenzo they need some money for groceries.

I leave the room and head into the kitchen. Angel is sitting on the floor rearranging some things on the bottom shelf.

"This place looks great."

She looks up. Her hair is coming loose from her ponytail and falling around her face. She blows it out of her face, but it doesn't work. I kneel down and move the stray hair from her face and tuck it in behind her ear.

"You look very beautiful when you're messy."

"Are you trying to get out of work? Because it's working," she laughs.

I bend down and kiss the top of her nose. "No, Beauty, just stating the facts. I'm going to help Donovan hang curtains."

"Don't mess them up or hang them crooked."

"Wouldn't dream of it."

We work on separate rooms and help out when asked by someone. I am shocked to see the progress we are making. Bruce, Vincenzo, John, Roger, Donovan, and I start taking empty boxes down to the garage. The girls pull up and we start to carry groceries into the house. They smile and talk with excitement when they see the progress of the house.

"This place looks lovely; it'll be perfect for Brea, Vincent, and baby Arturo," Selena cries.

"Oh, Lord, we forgot all about the baby's room," Doris cries.

"Oh, how awful. How did we forget about baby Arturo's room?" Selena shakes her head. "I feel just terrible."

"I'm sorry, I didn't tell you. That was the first room Vincent wanted done before they moved in. It's a surprise for Brea. Would you like to see it?" Angel asks softly, almost as if she is embarrassed.

"Oh, heavens, yes, we would love to, but where is it?" Doris asks, looking around the house.

"It's in the master bedroom. He wanted to use the sitting area as a nursery until the baby was old enough to be in his own room."

I watch as everyone goes upstairs to see the nursery. The guys head to the kitchen. There is beer and wine and platters of sandwiches and vegetables out on the counter.

Vincenzo tells me he has the item that Angel wanted for the nursery. He says it's in the basement and he'll be over tomorrow to help her with it. I have no idea what he is talking about, so I nod. When I open my second beer, Angel comes down the stairs, smiling.

She walks up to me and wraps her arms around me. "This place looks amazing," she says as she looks around.

"Yes, it does."

"Angel, you must be starving; please eat something," Roger says.

"Thank you, I will."

Angel says to me, "I'll be right back. Do you need anything?"

"No, Beauty, I'm fine."

Angel touches my arm lightly and walks away from me. I turn around so I can watch her. She gets stopped by several people as she fills her plate. She laughs and smiles freely. I take a drink of my beer and watch her. She looks up at me and I wink at her. She smiles and quickly looks away.

"She is one of a kind."

I look over and Vincenzo is standing next to me.

"I think so, too."

"You saw how quickly she got this place in shape."

I look around the fully furnished house, complete with draperies.

"She's a go-getter. I like that about her," he says as he walks away.

I take another drink of my beer and Angel comes over and stands next to me. She hands me another beer. The girls all come down the stairs chatting about the nursery and how beautiful it is. Once everyone has eaten and everything is cleaned up, we get ready to head home. Brea's Mom, Dad, and sisters are staying at Vincent and Brea's new house. Vincenzo tells Angel he'll meet her here tomorrow at noon to help with the nursery.

We invite Maria to stay with us, but she declines. Angel tells her we'll pick her up tomorrow morning for breakfast.

Angel

We get home, shower, and go right to bed. It has been a long time since we got any sleep, and we have been working hard. I get as close to Mason as I can in bed. He snuggles up to me, wraps his arms around me, and then kisses the top of my head.

"Are you all right?" he whispers into the top of my head.

"Better than ever," I say, looking up at him. "I just want to be close to you, tonight."

"I like that. I want to be this close to you every night," he says, kissing the top of my head again.

I fall into a dreamless sleep wrapped safely in Mason's arms. I swear I dream of his scent in my sleep.

I wake up to the smell of coffee and bacon. I hear someone in the shower and I also hear someone in the kitchen. I sit up in bed not sure who all is here. I hear female voices out in the kitchen and hear Mason singing in the shower. I smile. I love when Mason sings. He has such a soft, sweet voice. I remember yesterday: Aunt Maria's arrival and baby Arturo's birth. I climb out of bed and dress quickly in a tank top and yoga pants. I open the bedroom door and see Aunt Maria and Josephine in the kitchen, standing near the stove.

"Well, what a pleasant surprise." I beam.

"Pumpkin, good morning. I hope we didn't wake you."

"Nope, not at all. Good morning. I have to pee and brush my teeth," I say, walking through the living room into the guest bath. "Be right back. Good morning, Josephine."

"Good morning, dear." I hear them laughing.

After I wash my hands, I head out into the kitchen where a cup of hot coffee is waiting for me. I walk over and give Aunt Maria a big hug before hugging Josephine. I am so happy to have them both here. They are smiling and cooking breakfast together in Mason's house. This feels just perfect.

"May I help with something?"

"No, Pumpkin. Go sit down and drink your coffee. Another five minutes and it'll be ready."

"I'll be right back. I'm going to make the bed then."

I walk in the bedroom and the bathroom door is slightly open. I peek in and see Mason standing at the sink with a towel wrapped around his waist. He often opens the bathroom door after his shower to let the steam out. I just stand there and watch him brush his teeth. The muscles on his back and on his triceps flex. I should be making the bed, but I just stand there and watch him. The steam dissipates in the bathroom, and Mason smiles at me in the mirror.

"See something you like, Beauty?" He laughs.

Damn, he caught me ogling him, and he is using my line that I once said to him. *Think, Angel, think.*

"Nope, just looking to see who was making all the racket in here."

I turn around quickly so he can't see the blush on my face. I make the bed quickly and go back to the kitchen where Josephine and Aunt Maria are. I open the cabinets and begin setting the table. I move quickly without looking at anyone. I will the blush to go away from my face.

Mason strolls out of the bedroom wearing a pair of jeans — *nothing else*, just jeans. I look up at him; he is barefoot, no shirt, hair still wet and unruly. He smiles that All-American dimpled smile of his and I look away. He knows he got to me and he is going to use it to his advantage.

"Are you all right, dear?" Josephine asks, sweetly. I can feel the blush on my face. I only nod in her direction.

Mason walks over to me and whispers so only I can hear. "Racket, huh? You call my singing racket?" He smiles.

Game on, Handsome. I look up, smile brightly and stand a little taller. "I'm fine, Josephine. Thank you. I'm still tired, that's all. Someone was in the bathroom singing off key early this morning. I have a slight headache, that's all."

Mason chuckles, "Are you referring to me, Angel?" he says, as he clears his throat.

I look around the room. Maria and Josephine are laughing as they carry the food to the table.

"Well, since you're the only one who showered, I guess I am referring to you, Mason. It would be nice if you waited until everyone is awake before you try singing in the shower the next time. You were a little off key; you were not quite making the high notes, or the low notes — or the notes in the middle."

"Mmm, off key, huh. I'll try to keep it down from now on." He takes the towel he is holding and dries his hair while walking back into the bedroom, humming, His muscles flex as he moves the towel to dry his hair. *Damn him*. I can't help but watch until he is out of view.

I take a seat at the table and Mason re-enters fully dressed in his signature white linen shirt. He is still barefoot, which is very distracting. He smiles as he takes the seat beside me. Mason fills my plate and then his plate after Maria and Josephine fill theirs. I pour orange juice for everyone and we begin to eat.

Mason hums softly at the table and I smile, although I try hard not to.

Mason tells us there is a chance Brea will be released from the hospital later today.

"What? They are going to let her go home today?"

"Yes, typically 24 hours after the birth of a baby is all they keep you."

"A woman pushes a baby out the opening the size of a nostril and she gets to rest for only 24 hours? How will she get around? Can 24 hours possibly be long enough? Who is going to care for Arturo?"

"Oh, Pumpkin, she'll be fine. She'll *walk*, that's how she'll get around and *she'll* care for Arturo. If she needs help, her Mom, Dad, and sisters are there, not to mention Vincent," Aunt Maria says.

"She can walk? Are you sure?"

"Beauty, Vincent called me and said she wants to come home now. He is having a hard time keeping her in bed as it is."

"I had no idea," I say, eating the last piece of bacon on my plate. "The house isn't ready yet. Do we have any plans for today?" I say, looking to Mason.

"You need to meet with Vincenzo about something he made for Junior at noon. I thought you could stay at the house while I go and pick Brea up from the hospital and bring them home. That way, you'll have time to put the finishing touches on the house."

"Finishing touches, I have more than finishing touches to do. I'll shower as soon as I help clean up."

"Angel, we'll clean up, and you go and get ready." Josephine smiles.

"What are your plans today? Do you want to go with us to Vincent and Brea's house?"

"Oh, no, Pumpkin, that sounds like too much fun for us." Aunt Maria laughs. "Josephine and I are going to play bingo at the church this morning."

"Oh, that's nice. Did you drive over here this morning?"

"Josephine and I were having coffee this morning when Mason called and asked if I was ready for him to come and get me. Josephine didn't have anything planned for today, so we thought we would come over here and have breakfast with you two before we went to bingo."

"I'm so glad you did. Bingo sounds like fun. I didn't know you played bingo," I say honestly.

"Oh, yes, I love playing Bingo. It's so exciting to yell 'Bingo.' You and Mason need to come with us one day."

I look over at Mason and he has his brow raised, shaking his head at me.

"We would love to. The sooner the better." I laugh. *Bingo, I got him,* I think to myself.

Once I have showered, I say my goodbyes to Josephine and Aunt Maria. Mason and I pick up a few items from the store before we head over to Brea and Vincent's new house. The house is busy with Brea's sisters running the sweeper and mopping. Vincenzo, John, Doris, and Selena are up in the nursery, so Mason and I go up there.

Vincenzo is placing the handmade wooden baby cradle near the master bed. He swings it lightly to check for squeaks and to make sure it swings smoothly. I let out an 'aww' and he looks up at me and smiles.

My eyes tear up. "That is so beautiful. I can't believe you made that by hand." I walk over to the cradle and swing it softly. A small music box inside the cradle plays "Jesus Loves Me."

Selena and Doris also have tears in their eyes. "It's amazing, isn't it?" Selena says.

"Oh, it is. I had no idea how talented you are," I say, looking over at Vincenzo.

"At one time I would have stained it; but now they say that the fumes from the stain are bad for the baby. I like the natural wood color," he says, swinging the cradle again.

"I love it just like it is; I think it's perfect."

Mason clears his throat and asks, "Has Vincent called yet?"

"Hi, Mason. He called and said they'll be ready at three."

I look at my watch, "I better get busy."

I head into the nursery and get a clean cradle-sized sheet from the dresser with a soft blue blanket. I go to the cradle and wind up the small music box again. After making the bed, I re-position the cradle so it will be perfect for them to view upon entry into the bedroom. Everyone leaves, and Mason walks up behind me and hums, "Jesus Loves Me." I stand and lean back into him. I love his singing and move slightly side to side with the music.

"We could have this as 'our song' at *our* wedding," he laughs.

I turn around to face him, "As much as I love this song, we need something a little more romantic. I was hoping you would sing to me at our wedding."

He laughs, "So you can insult me again? Never. What was that you said earlier? I sounded like I was making racket and was off key?"

"It was racket and you *were* off key," I lie. "We are getting married at nighttime so you'll have time to condition your throat or voice, or whatever it is people condition."

"Mmm, I do like the song 'Brickhouse' by the Commodores. Have you ever heard it? With practice I may be able…."

"Oh, no, you don't. Don't even joke about that." I laugh.

"Would I do that to you?"

"Um, yeah. Yeah, I do believe you would. Don't you have someone to pick up at the hospital?"

Mason leans down to kiss me before he leaves. "I do need to get going. I'll be home shortly with the Salvatore family."

"Drive safely and hurry. I can't wait to get my hands on Arturo."

Mason smiles and walks out the room singing "Brickhouse" by the Commodores.

I laugh and he looks back at me and winks before he disappears down the hallway.

Mason gets the base of the car seat fastened correctly in the center of the backseat of Vincent's truck. Sara, Sylvia, and Donovan pull up and Donovan rides to the hospital with Mason. Everyone else stays behind and gets the house and some food ready for Arturo's homecoming. Selena and Doris strategically places hand sanitizer throughout the house. *Good thinking.*

Sara and I do a walkthrough of the house and it looks amazing. Hard to believe we did all this in a matter of two days. It's wonderful to have so many people pitching in to help. I am so blessed to be part of this amazing group of people, of this family. I look at my watch.

"We should start getting the food ready."

"I think they already did that," Sara says as she walks down the stairs with me.

I hear a truck pull up outside and my heart begins to beat a little faster. I am so excited to see them.

"Oh, my God, they are already here," Sara squeals.

I run down the stairs, trying to keep up with Sara. The front door is already standing open. We walk out onto the front porch to join everyone already out there. Everyone is smiling and waving as the truck stops. The grandfathers are already in the yard waiting to assist Brea and carry her suitcase.

John helps Brea get out of the tall truck. She is wearing sweat pants and a tee shirt. She looks amazing. Her red hair is in a high ponytail and she has her makeup done perfectly. She stands tall and waits for John to get the baby out of the truck. Vincent takes the baby from John, and they walk up the front porch together. I stand there with my mouth open.

"What's wrong with you?"

"Nothing, you look amazing."

"Thanks, I feel great."

"That didn't hurt?"

"What? Birth?"

"Yeah, birth."

"Oh, that hurt like a bitch. Vincent will be lucky if we ever share a bed together again. But we do have an amazing son out of it."

Laughing, I follow her inside.

"Wow, this place looks amazing. I was shocked when Mason said we were coming here."

Vincent and Brea look around and smile.

"This is amazing. You guys must have worked non-stop to get everything done on time. Vincent and I can't thank you enough," Brea says, wiping the tears from her cheek.

"Please tell me you didn't bring Vincent's nasty recliner." Brea looks around the house.

"Sure did, we put it in his mancave." Mason laughs.

Vincent turns around, "Mancave, I have a mancave? Hell, yeah!" He grins.

"Vincent, you do not have a mancave," Brea says sternly.

"Brea, this house is twice as big as our other one. Most of what I didn't get rid of before you moved in, you got rid of when you got there. All I want is a room: one room and my chair. You can have the rest of the house to do with as you wish."

"One room and your stinky chair stays in there."

Vincent walks over and hugs her, "That is why I love you."

He thought, *I'm glad Brea doesn't know about my collection of vintage Ramones tee shirts and torn blue jeans. I'll start wearing them soon, I hope ... after Brea stops being embarrassed when I hear her fart.*

"Do you want to see the nursery?" I ask Brea, excitedly.

"You had time to do the nursery?"

"I've been working on it for a few days. Vincent wanted it done, first."

She looks up at Vincent, "You did?"

He winks at her. "I wanted our son to have a place to sleep, and I didn't want you to worry about getting it ready."

"Let's go see it. I haven't seen what it looks like yet," Vincent says, looking at Brea.

"I hope you like it. I think I may have maxed out your credit card. The last transaction declined," I say.

Vincent stops dead in his tracks and his face falls.

I walk past him. "Come on, I'm just kidding."

Vincent kisses the baby and hands the baby off to Vincenzo before we walk up the stairs. Mason and I wait while Vincent and Brea walk into the master bedroom first.

"This is our room. I want to see the nursery first," Brea says softly.

Vincent opens the door and turns on the light. Mason and I follow behind them. The handmade cradle is beside the bed. Brea lets out a cry and Vincent walks her over to it.

"Did your Dad do this?" she asks, sitting on the edge of the bed and rocking the cradle side to side.

"He did." Vincent reaches inside and turns the music box on. It plays "Jesus Loves Me" and she cries again.

Mason wraps his arm around me and holds me to him. I rest my hand on his shoulder and watch Brea and Vincent. They are so sweet together. He touches her gingerly as she cries.

"It's all right, cupcake."

"Is that grandma's music box?"

"Your Mom wanted Arturo to have it."

Brea sniffles and continues to cry.

"Do you want to see the nursery?" Vincent asks.

"I thought this was the surprise. Vincent, I want Arturo to sleep in here with us. If his nursery is down the hall, that will be too far away. I won't hear him cry all the way down there."

Vincent stands and takes Brea's hands without saying a word. She stands as she clings to him. They walk the short distance around the corner of the room to the sitting area. Mason and I follow quietly.

Vincent opens the door and turn on the light switch. The pale blue lamp with the sailboat lampshade gives the room a soft glow. The baby bed is placed on the left side of the room with the changing table beside it. To the right corner of the room is a white plush oversized rocking chair and ottoman. Above the large bay window is a pale blue valance with more sailboats. The window was left untreated, as Vincent requested. He wanted the baby to have a view of the wooded land and wildlife behind the house. The baby bedding is also done in sailboats along with a matching mobile. Brea walks over and winds the mobile up. It plays "Jesus Loves Me." I look up at Mason and he shrugs. That isn't the song it played when I bought it. Brea starts to cry and Vincent holds her. She walks around the room looking at all the pictures of her and Vincent in the picture frames that are scattered around the room. There are even some pictures of Arturo that Vincent took.

Brea turns around and hugs me. "I love it! I love everything!"

"Good, I was afraid you wouldn't. Maybe it wasn't childish enough or young enough for him."

"Are you kidding, the way Vincent loves to sail? This is perfect."

Mason

The next couple weeks Angel fills in at the insurance company while Brea is on maternity leave. She also meets with Marilyn, her new client, a few times a week and stores specialty items in the garage that comes in for Marilyn's lanai. The renovation needs to be completed in three weeks. Angel stresses about making the deadline, although everything she has ordered has arrived on time.

The condo sold, so I will be closing on that next week. Madison got more than I expected out of it, so I couldn't be happier. I am also glad it sold in such a short amount of time.

Brea, Vincent, and Arturo mostly stay home. Her sisters and parents have returned to Ohio so Brea and Vincent are trying to get into a routine as a family. We have stopped over with dinner a few times and occasionally call to offer support.

Tonight Angel and I are meeting Sara, Donovan, and Emma, who is the new girl at the insurance company, at Geicko's for dinner and drinks. Angel likes Emma and is excited for me to meet her.

"Are you sure this looks all right?" Angel asks, walking into the kitchen.

I look up at her; she is adjusting the sleeves on her shirt. She is wearing jeans, a white blouse, and heels. Her hair is long and straight; red lipstick and gold hoop earrings complete her outfit.

"What?" she asks.

I blink a few times; I didn't realize I was staring.

"I'm changing."

"Wait, why?"

"Because you are just looking at me, that's why."

I down the rest of my Scotch and walk over to her.

"Beauty," I say, cupping her face in my hands. "I was staring at you because you are unbelievably beautiful." I kiss the tip of her nose. "I didn't say anything because how do you tell someone they are the most beautiful thing you have ever seen?"

She smiles and wraps her arms around my neck. She stands on her tiptoes and kisses me. "You always know exactly what to say. Thank you."

I lift her off the ground and kiss her back. "I only speak the truth. You are beautiful."

We are the first to arrive at the restaurant, and we decide to sit at a highball table in the bar. The music is low as we order our drinks. Angel decides on a mint mohito and I have a Corona with lime. We sip our drinks and Angel fills me in on Emma. She tells me that Emma is a single mom of a four-year-old son and that she lives in a small house in Sarasota. Angel says that Emma is a single mom who doesn't date or get out much. Other than work, she is completely devoted to her son. I find it difficult to speak and just nod.

I have never asked about the new girl in Sara and Brea's office before. When I finally find my voice, I ask about Emma's family. I learn that her mother and father live in the area; that was the only information Angel had.

Angel stands and waves at a small petite blond entering the front door. She is wearing jeans, a tee shirt, and sandals. When the woman sees Angel, she smiles and waves back. I stand and wait for the two to say their hellos. Angel walks Emma to the table and introduces us. We all sit and Emma orders a glass of white wine. I sit back and listen while Angel and Emma talk. Angel tries to include me in the conversation every now and then.

I look at the front door and see a colleague of mine walk in: Alec Collins. Alec was Angel's doctor when she was in the hospital. He sees me and smiles before walking over in our direction. I stand and we shake hands. I introduce him to Angel and Emma as if he and Angel have never met. He remembers Angel but Angel, of course, doesn't remember him. It's a story for another time. He doesn't say anything and I know he understands.

I wave to the bartender to get Alec a drink and for another round of drinks for us.

I notice Alec look over at the girls a few times. I'm not sure if he's looking at Emma, or at Angel. The last time he saw Angel she was battered and beaten.

"Alec, why don't you join us for dinner?' Angel asks.

I think she may be playing matchmaker, but it's too soon to tell. I see Emma look at her watch, but she doesn't say anything. I also look at my phone for the time. Sara and Donovan are already late.

He looks at Angel and then stares at Emma. "I only came in for a drink, but dinner sounds great. Are you sure?" he asks, looking at Emma.

Angel smiles and says, "We would love for you to stay."

I sit across from Angel and Alec sits across from Emma. Sara and Donovan walk in all giddy. Alec and I stand until they reach our table.

"Sorry we're late. Sara started drinking early and didn't want to leave the house."

Sara hugs Emma, then Angel. Donovan pulls a chair out for Sara and she sits down. Donovan winks at her before sitting beside her at the round highball table. After they order their drinks, we look over the menu and decide on dinner. I made sure the bartender knew to put everything on one check. I have no idea what Emma's financial status is, but if I can lighten her load, I will.

We order dinner and Emma orders a side salad and soup. Because she is a single mother, I'm sure her finances are tight. I look at the appetizers and order several different ones. Angel looks at me.

"I'm hungry."

We all talk about Brea and Vincent's baby, the insurance business, and the hospital. Alec tells us they have been extremely busy. Angel looks over at Alec and I think it has registered, she knows him. He tips his beer bottle towards her, nods, and continues talking. Emma talks about working with Sara and Brea but doesn't mention a husband or her son.

We eat and have a great time together. We say our goodbyes and head home.

While driving home, Angel asks, "I know Alec, don't I?"

"He was your doctor when you were in Intensive Care."

"He's a friend of yours?"

"He was my colleague at the hospital. I like him, but I have never associated with him outside of work before now. I'm not sure 'friend' is a word I would use."

"I like him. We should invite him to our wedding."

"We can do that." I look over at her and smile.

"You're planning something. Does it have to do with Emma?"

"Maybe."

Angel

"Mason, come on, they're here," I yell, rushing to the front door. I open the door and wait on the porch for Vincent and Brea to get the baby from the back of the truck. I am so excited. This is the first night for us to babysit. Vincent wants a date night with Brea and Mason, and I get to babysit. Mason stands behind me and wraps his arms around my waist.

"Do you think they brought enough diapers?" Mason whispers in my ear. We watch as Vincent grabs a very large diaper bag from the back seat. "Arturo seems to be a poop machine."

I whisper back, "All babies are."

I open the door wide for Brea and wider for Vincent to walk through. He is carrying Arturo in a baby carrier and has the diaper bag slung over his left shoulder.

Vincent sets the baby down near the couch, and I sit in the rocking chair. Brea hands me the baby, and I automatically smell him. He smells so good.

"There are diapers, wipes, burp cloths, a couple changes of clothes, and some bottles in the insulated pouches. Make sure you change his diaper every hour and feed him every two hours. The bottles are filled with breast milk, so make sure Mason doesn't taste it."

"Whoa, whoa, wait a minute. And why would you think I would taste your breast milk?"

"Sometimes people taste it to check the temperature of the milk. Just put some on your wrist to check the temperature."

"Don't worry," Mason says while walking over to stand near Vincent.

I cuddle the baby and inhale him again.

"Vincent, I'm not sure I can leave him yet," Brea says, sitting on the couch near the rocking chair.

Vincent walks over and kneels down in front of her. "Cupcake, it's just for a couple hours. I just want some alone time with my girl. Just you and me, alone; just the two of us." He lifts her head gently with his fingers so she can see him. "Just you and me."

"Ok, two hours?"

"No more, I promise. They are our friends and they will care for him as we would. I just want some alone time with you, with no interruptions." He leans in and kisses her sweetly.

She nods and stands up. They both kiss the baby before leaving. Mason closes the door after them and has a sour look on his face.

"What's wrong with you?"

"I'm still thinking about what Brea said about me tasting her breast milk. I actually prefer beer. May I hold him?" Mason says, holding his hands out for Arturo.

I rearrange the baby and hand him to Mason. Mason sits on the couch, removes the blanket from the baby, and holds him out so he can see him better. Mason smiles and kisses Arturo on his forehead before turning him over. Mason looks at him, feels his spine, and turns him back around.

"Mason, are you assessing him or holding him?"

"I'm just holding him." Mason touches his head and feels his intelligence bump.

I stand up and remove a diaper, a burp cloth, wipes, and a bottle from the diaper bag.

"It looks like you are assessing him to me. Here, let me have him, he's fine."

Mason wraps him back up in the soft blue blanket and hands him back to me. "He sure is." Mason kisses the baby on the forehead before handing him to me.

I change him then feed him. Mason sits on the couch and watches. He usually has a beer or a Scotch by now but tonight he is drinking water. Mason's phone dings that he has an incoming text. He pulls his phone from his back pocket and laughs. "It's Vincent, Brea went to the restroom and he's checking on Junior," Mason says as he replies.

I also have a text. "It's Brea, she snuck to the restroom to check on Junior — I mean Arturo."

We both laugh and take turns holding the baby. Mason is so relaxed holding him. He always kisses the baby on the forehead and never on the lips. I know it's because he is afraid of spreading germs to the baby. I always hold Arturo close so I can smell him. I'm beginning to wonder if I have a problem smelling people. First Mason, now Arturo.

Brea and Vincent walk in and almost fight over who will hold the baby first. Mason and I laugh at the way they cuddle him.

"How was your date?" I ask.

"It was good, but we missed our little man," Brea says in her baby voice I have never heard before.

"It was great; we were able to talk about the wedding, just the two of us. So many people are involved and everyone has an opinion," Vincent states.

"I can see how that would be a problem. What did you two come up with?" I ask, walking over to sit near Mason.

"My wedding dress for one. Since I chose it while I was pregnant, Mom thinks I should go with a different style. I loved it when I got it and I still love it. I go in for the final fitting Wednesday. Can you believe the wedding is in two weeks?"

"I can't, time is flying by. Look at how much different things are now. You have a baby." I smile.

"Not just a baby, I have the most cutest lil man in the whole world," Brea says, using her baby voice again. "What about your wedding dress? Have you thought much about it?" Brea asks in a normal tone.

"I am hoping to wear my mother's wedding dress. Uncle Raùl is bringing it down with him when he comes. It'll need cleaned and altered. My mother was very slim, so I'm not sure I can wear it at all."

Mason nods, but doesn't say anything.

Vincent and Brea also talk about their honeymoon. They didn't plan one since Brea would have just delivered. But since Arturo decided to come early and will be six weeks old at the wedding, Vincent would like to take them someplace beautiful and relaxing.

Once they are gone, Mason and I talk about our own honeymoon. I have never traveled and I am really a pretty simple girl. I don't have any dream places I want to see. Just some intimate alone time with Mason is all I want.

"We never talked about your wedding dress before. I think it will be nice for you to wear your mother's wedding dress."

"You do? Aren't you afraid it'll be too old fashioned?"

"No, not at all. I think it will be perfect. You know, we have never talked about wedding rings either."

"No, I guess we haven't. I assumed you would buy mine and I would buy yours."

"I was thinking, I would like to take care of the rings and plan the honeymoon. You can plan the wedding."

"I was going to plan the wedding anyway," I joke. "What do you have in mind for the rings and honeymoon?"

"Nothing planned yet, but I do have some ideas."

"Mason, you have to promise me, nothing extravagant. No big flashy rings and no over-the-top honeymoon."

"I can do that. Nothing flashy and nothing over the top."

It's Thursday and I kiss Mason goodbye. My client, Marilyn, is out of town, but I need to put the last finishing touches in the lanai. The luau is scheduled for next weekend, and I am ahead of schedule, thanks to an early delivery of the furniture. I drive my loaded-down SUV and let myself in using the key she left for me.

The waterfall has been installed and looks beautiful dead center on the focal point wall straight ahead. It can be seen anywhere from the lanai. The gas fireplace has been built out of stone and is elegant on the opposite wall of the waterfall. The delivery for the live indoor plants arrived right on schedule. I arrange the tall indoor trees and plants, add the lighting to the base of them, and fluff the pale yellow and green pillows on the outdoor furniture.

I turn on the gas fireplace with the light switch and it comes on and off as it's supposed to. I turn the waterfall on and off the same way and am pleased it works without difficulty. I turn everything on including the new bamboo ceiling fans and walk around the pool. I snap some pictures for my portfolio and leave a thank-you gift — a bottle of champagne — and the house key on the kitchen island.

Marilyn, Thank you for giving me the opportunity to design an area in your home. I personally love it. The waterfall and gas fireplace were excellent additions. I was able to complete it sooner than expected. It was wonderful working with you, and I hope you get many years of enjoyment from it. Angel.

I also leave a case of white pillar candles with instructions of where to place them the night of the luau. If I put them out now, the Florida heat will surely melt them. Even in October it's very warm.

I get a call from Marilyn telling me she is expecting to see me and Mason at her luau. She thanks me for my small thank-you gift and tells me that is her favorite brand of champagne. I promise Mason and I will be there and I am looking forward to it.

It's the night of the luau and I bought Mason and me something special to wear. When he is in the shower, I lay his clothes out on the bed. Happy with my decision, I go into the guest bedroom and change. When I put the last finishing touches on, I walk out into the lanai, where I know Mason will be. He is watching the dolphins feeding and has his back to me. He is wearing the white linen pants, the white floral Hawaiian shirt, and the tan Sperrys I bought him. He has a glass of wine already poured and sitting on the outside table, waiting for me.

I take the wine, walk over to him, and wrap my arm around his waist. "You look very Hawaiian tonight," I smile.

He looks down at his shirt. "Thank you, my fiancé has excellent taste."

"I like the way that sounds."

"I like 'wife' better, but I'll settle for 'fiancé' for now. You look very Hawaiian yourself," he says, twirling me around.

I decided on a white dress with very large colorful flowers. It matches Mason's shirt but isn't identical.

"Do you think it's too much?"

"No, I think it's very appropriate for tonight. Are you ready?"

"I am."

We arrive at the party and are greeted warmly. "Welcome, darling, and this must be your very handsome Mason Myles."

"Hello, Marilyn. Marilyn, I would like to introduce Mason Myles. Mason, this is Marilyn Wilson."

"Oh, Mason, it's very nice to finally meet you. I have heard some wonderful things about you."

"Likewise, Mrs. Wilson, and thank you. You have a very lovely home."

"No, no, please cut the formalities, just call me Marilyn."

"Ok, Marilyn."

"First put these on," she says, handing us leis. "Then go outside and get yourselves a drink. Mason, look around at the fabulous job Angel has done. You wouldn't believe the before and after. The space is absolutely stunning."

"Ok, thank you, we will."

"And I have had people wanting to know who my designer is. So you'll be meeting future clients as well. Just tell them you are already booked up for the next year." Marilyn winks.

We enter the room and Mason automatically waves to someone in the other room. I look around; other than

Marilyn and Mason, I don't know anyone. We walk outside to the bar and see Julia standing there. Mason holds me closer and continues to his destination. I love that Mason backs down to no one.

Mason orders us two glasses of champagne. I wait for Julia to come over, but she doesn't. To my surprise she leaves the room, alone.

Mason takes my hand and leads me to a sitting area near the lit fireplace.

"Here, Beauty. Are you cold?" he asks, handing me my glass of champagne.

"No, I'm fine. The fire feels nice."

"She is right," Mason says, while looking around the lanai.

"About what?"

"You are very talented."

"I can't take all the credit; this place didn't need that much work to begin with. It was already beautiful the way it was."

Mason and I walk around and dance to the Hawaiian music playing on the surround sound. We eat a variety of Hawaiian appetizers and dishes like Laulau, Kalua Pig, Poke, and Pineapple. Marilyn went all out on the caterer. The Hawaiian dishes were delicious.

I laugh and smile so much my cheeks begin to hurt.

Several people come over to Mason and he introduces me. I will never be able to remember everyone.

Mason and I are standing at the bar with another couple when Marilyn comes up to us with Julia. I turn around and almost choke.

"Are you all right, Angel?"

"I'm sorry, yes, I'm fine. The drink is a little strong, that's all."

"Julia just told me she had to meet my designer so I had to introduce you. Julia Johnson, this is my personal designer and friend, Angel Perez, and this is her beau, Mason Myles. Angel and Mason, this is Julia Johnson. Julia is one of the best attorneys around. I swear she can get the guilty to be found innocent."

Now it's Mason's turn to choke.

I reach my hand out for Julia's. I can play this game. "It's nice to meet you. So you like my work?" *Ha, there you go.*

Julia barely touches my hand to shake it. "Yes, it's very unique."

"Now, Julia, you were just saying how much you loved her work and how you were looking for someone with her taste." Marilyn smiles.

"Yes, I supposed I did. You do have exquisite taste. What was your name again? Was it Angie?"

Mason clears his throat and takes a step forward. I reach my arm out to let me know I am all right. "No, it's Angel. If you'll excuse us, I promised my fiancé the next slow dance," I say, taking Mason by the hand.

"Now don't forget, I have Angel booked up for the next year, so don't try to steal her from me, Julia. I know how you work," Marilyn laughs.

"No, Marilyn, I wouldn't think of it. Angel, you do great work and it was very nice meeting you and Mason." Julia nods and walks away.

Mason leads me to the dance floor and holds me close. "That went better than I thought."

"It did, you must have put the fear of God in her."

"Well, nobody wants to lose something they worked so hard to get."

"Can you really get her debarred?"

"I don't know, but I'll die trying and she knows it."

"Thank you."

On the drive home from the party, Mason and I laugh the entire drive back. I was worried I wouldn't fit in, but I did. We both had a lot of fun. Mason knew a lot of the people there, so that was nice.

"Mason, did you happen to use the restroom while you were there?"

"I did, why?"

"Because, every time I went to the restroom red rose petals were floating in the toilet."

We both laugh and I know I have had too much to drink. He introduced me to more people than I can remember. Marilyn didn't know Mason but has heard of his family. The Myles family name has a great reputation in the area. Everyone either knows them or has heard of them.

CHAPTER FOUR: SOMETHING OLD, SOMETHING NEW, SOMETHING BORROWED, SOMETHING BLUE

Mason

Once we are done and the wedding rehearsal is over, we head over to Ruth's Chris Steakhouse for the rehearsal dinner.

When dinner is over, Brea cries and Vincent tries to comfort her. I know it's the emotions of the wedding. We all say our goodbyes and head home. Angel, Sara, and Brea are staying at Brea's with Arturo, while Vincent and Donovan are staying at my place. Some rule about it being bad luck for the bride and groom to see each other before the wedding.

Angel texts me to let me know they have arrived home safely. Once we are home, Donovan opens a new bottle of Scotch.

"Here's to the good life," Donovan says, holding up his glass.

"Cheers," Vincent and I say in unison as we clink our glasses together. We drink until the bottle is empty. *Thank God for a late wedding tomorrow,* I think to myself.

We wake up and nurse our hangovers until noon. Coffee and Tylenol make a sure fix. Once we are feeling better, we shower and get ready for the day. Vincent has some running around to do before the wedding. Vincent made some changes in the wedding plans and wants to surprise Brea. We shop at a few specialty shops to see if they can help him. He stops by Jared's Jewelry Store to pick up Brea's wedding gift from him and then he goes by Toys R Us to get a wedding gift for Arturo: a box set of 12 rattles. I can't help but smile. They even gift-wrapped it for him in pale blue paper.

We shower and have a drink or two before heading to the Sarasota Botanical Gardens. Vincent tugs on his bowtie and stretches his neck side to side.

"You're not choking, you know," I say.

"I feel like I am." He coughs and moves his head side to side again.

We arrive and see Brea's car parked in the front. We begin to get out of the car, but Vincent doesn't move. Donovan looks at me and I look at Vincent.

"What's up?" I ask.

"It just dawned on me tonight I am marrying the woman of my dreams."

"You are a lucky bastard," I say in all seriousness.

He looks over and smiles. "I am, aren't I?"

"Come on, let's go so you can claim your girl," Donovan says.

We walk to the reception center at the Botanical Gardens and are greeted by the preacher, Kenneth Kettlewell.

"Brea is already here," he says, smiling.

"Is our son with her?"

"He is; would you like me to get him for you?"

"Please, I have missed him. I'll also need someplace to change him, please."

"We have a room set up for you and the male wedding party, just give me a minute."

We walk around the reception area until we hear a baby's cry coming from down the hall. Vincent disappears and returns with a crying Arturo. He holds him to his chest and kisses him. Vincent bounces him and then whispers something to him before humming "Old Man River." The vibrating bass sound quiets Arturo.

"You can change him in here." We all walk into another more private room. Donovan removes the all-white outfit and starts removing the price tags from it. Vincent changes the baby's diaper and dresses him in his new white outfit. He holds the baby up and I smile.

"He looks like an angel," I say, honestly. His dark hair and his all-white outfit make me think that. A lump begins to form in my throat. Vincent is holding Arturo, who is fast asleep. We walk through the room and are greeted by a woman, the wedding coordinator, Phyllis Prince.

"Hello, Vincent, gentlemen. We are about to begin; please follow me."

We follow her out of the building and down a brick walkway, which is lined with white orchids. White twinkling lights are in all the trees. It's dusk and the lights are just now showing up. We continue to walk through a flower-filled garden illuminated by candles and more twinkling lights. The aroma of fresh flowers fills the air.

We enter into an open garden where the water fountain is also illuminated by lighting in the water. I have never been here at night — it is breathtaking. Hundreds of chairs are lined up and filled with Brea's and Vincent's family and friends. We make our way to the front and stand near the white, floral, lit archway.

Vincent

I'm standing in front of the room holding my son. All eyes are on us. I feel like I am going to choke. I'll never understand why anyone would choose to wear a monkey suit for a living. Arturo begins to fuss, so I hold him closer to me. He smells like Brea. He always smells like Brea. I kiss his dark fly-away hair again and he calms. I calm. I turn slightly and I can see Donovan, Mason, and my three cousins standing beside me all calm and in control. I feel like I'm going to lose it. I am marrying the woman of my dreams and I can't wait. I just want to marry her and make her mine. I'm nervous and I have no idea why.

The music begins to play and I look down the aisle. Our flower girl, Sophia, walks out first. She is Brea's two-year-old cousin. She is wearing a white dress with red roses along the bottom with black shiny shoes. She drops red rose petals as she walks towards me. Everyone oohs and ahhs. She smiles and I can't help but smile back. She walks and stands in front of me. She looks up at me with her clear green eyes and red hair. I swear she looks like a baby doll.

Our ring bearer, Bryson, is next. He is my two-year-old nephew. He walks out wearing a black tux. He carries the silk pillow that holds our wedding rings on it. He doesn't smile. He probably feels like he's choking, too. He stops halfway down the aisle and plays with the red ribbon holding our wedding rings to the pillow. *Please don't untie that bow,* I think to myself. Everyone laughs and he startles. He hurries and stands beside Sophia.

Angel is next, then Brea's three sisters. They are all wearing the same long red formal dress. Sara comes out right before Brea; Sara's dress is a little different: same color, but off the shoulder. Once she is in place, the music changes.

Everyone stands and faces the back of the room. My heart beats faster. I feel like I can't breathe. This is Brea, the love of my life. I haven't been away from her for this long since I can't remember when. I haven't made love to her since before our son's birth just over six weeks ago. I turn Arturo around. I want him to see Brea as I see her. She steps out from behind the bushes, with her arms linked with her Dad's. Looking at her, I swear, she takes my breath away. She locks eyes with mine and stops. Tears fall onto her pale cheeks. I want to run up there and comfort her, but I smile instead. Her father whispers something into her ears and pats her on her hand.

She nods and begins to walk towards me. I watch my future wife take her last few steps as a single woman. The moment I make her mine can't come fast enough. Arturo fusses so I bounce him.

I can't wait any longer. I am supposed to meet them at the altar, but I walk to meet them. When I get to her, I take her hand. She smiles at me and leans in to kiss our son. She uses her fingers to wipe away the lipstick smudge from his small cheeks. I bend down to kiss her and she kisses me back.

Her father leans in and whispers, "That comes at the end of the ceremony."

I lean back away from Brea, smile, and say, "Sorry, I couldn't wait." Everyone laughs and Brea cries.

Her father kisses her and I walk her the short distance to stand in front of the preacher. I listen intently to what he says. When it is time to say our vows, I hand Arturo to Donovan. We repeat our vows and exchange rings. When it is time to kiss the bride, Brea steps back slightly.

"Slow" is all she says before she kisses me sweetly. Arturo cries and Brea looks around me and reaches for him. She kisses him and then turns around so we are facing our friends and family. The preacher introduces us as, "Mr. and Mrs. Vincent Antonio Salvatore *and Family."* Everyone laughs, Brea cries, and I stand tall and proud. *My family.*

Angel

The wedding reception is in full swing. The grandparents left to put Arturo to bed, and Brea and Vincent also left after they cut the cake. They are getting a hotel room tonight and then leaving with the baby tomorrow to honeymoon in the Smoky Mountains.

"One last dance, Beauty?" Mason whispers in my ear.

"I turn around and smile. "I would love to, Handsome."

He takes my hand and leads me to the dance floor; he holds me close. Mason holds my hand close to his heart and wraps his other arm around my waist. He is such a smooth dancer. I rest my head on his shoulder, and he kisses my cheek. He sings softly in my ear, and I swear I could melt. We sway to the music and I smile. I just listen to his soothing voice.

After the dance, we help with the cleanup, and Sara and Donovan walk over and announce they are leaving. The party is still going strong. Over a hundred people are still here. Brea's sisters are dancing with Vincent's cousins; they are laughing and having a great time.

"Are you ready?" Mason asks.

"Yes, I think so. Sara and I need to get our things first."

We walk to the reception building and are let into the dressing room. We gather our clothing, purses, makeup bags, and shoes before exiting the room. After saying our goodbyes, Mason and I drive home.

The next few days are filled with taking the gifts over to Brea and Vincent's house. I also received the nicest thank-you letter from my client, Marilyn:

Angel, Darling, I feel I didn't get a chance to appropriately thank you for your efforts on adding new life to my dreadful lanai. I didn't think it would ever be a space I truly loved, until now. The waterfall is my favorite, next to the lovely outdoor furniture. You are truly talented, and I would love for you to continue working your magic in the rest of my home. My master suite is in dire need of a facelift. Please call me when you have time so we can get this underway. You are truly a gifted and talented designer. Thank you again, Darling. Looking forward to seeing you soon. Marilyn

This is great news. I call her the next day and we decide to meet and discuss her ideas.

Uncle Raùl called and confirmed he will be down for Thanksgiving. He said he found Momma's dress and some other wedding items he will be bringing with him. I am excited to see him, the dress, and the other items he is talking about.

Mason and I are going to dinner tonight with Sara, Donovan, Brea, Vincent, and Arturo. We haven't seen them since they returned home from their honeymoon. We don't dress up but wear jeans and a sweater — the weather has finally cooled off and we can now wear long sleeves.

We are last to arrive and walk hand in hand into the crowded restaurant. We see everyone as soon as we walk in. Brea is holding Arturo, and he is smiling at her. Sara and Brea are talking to him while Vincent has his arm draped over the back of Brea's chair.

Donovan and Vincent stand when we near the table, Mason pulls my chair out for me. He shakes hands with Donovan and Vincent before sitting.

"So how was the honeymoon?" Sara asks.

"It was wonderful; we mostly just stayed in and relaxed. Vincent surprised us with a secluded cabin in the mountains. He even had it stocked with food and toiletry items we normally use. I have no idea who he got to shop for us, but they did a wonderful job. It was just like walking into our own home."

"Did you see any bears while you were there?" I ask excitedly.

"We did. We bought a picnic lunch from a cute little teahouse, called Magnolias. Then we drove through Cades Cove and ate outside on a blanket in one of the open fields. We were able to spot a family of bears in the distance," Brea answers, while bouncing Arturo on her lap.

"How was the honeymoon with the baby?" Mason asks, looking directly at Vincent.

"Great," is all Vincent says, smiling.

"We had a hot tub outside on the porch that overlooked the mountains. We were able to use that when the baby was asleep. It was even cool enough to use the indoor fireplace," Brea adds.

Brea and Vincent share pictures of the wedding and of their relaxing honeymoon, although it sounds more like a family vacation.

"This is a nice picture," Mason laughs, holding it up for everyone to see. The picture is of Vincent and Brea standing at the altar. Vincent has a chain with a large black ball around his ankle. "Ball and Chain."

We all laugh.

"It's great having photographers in the family. Don't stop there, there's more," Vincent nods towards the handful of pictures.

Another picture of Vincent and Brea showed them standing behind what looked like a jail cell.

Mason laughs again. "I didn't see Jerry Springer at your wedding," he says, holding up another picture of the wedding party where Jerry Springer photobombed it — or where someone Photoshopped him in. "The photos all look great — even the Photoshopped ones," Donovan says, laughing as he passes them around the table. "It may have actually been Jerry Springer since he has a home in Sarasota," Donovan adds.

"The photo where you are kneeling in church and your shoes have written on the soles HELP and ME were not Photoshopped," Mason says. "I used shoe polish to write those words."

We order dinner and pass the baby around. Mason still calls him Junior and Brea laughs. At one time she would have hurt him for calling him that.

A woman screams from a nearby table and we all look over. Mason stands immediately and rushes over and Vincent and Donovan are right behind him. I stand up but stand near our table. I watch the commotion, but I'm not sure what's going on.

I hear someone yell, "She's choking! Call 911!"

I reach for my phone and call 911.

"Nine, one, one. What is your emergency?"

"I'm in a restaurant and someone is choking," I stutter.

"What is your exact location, ma'am?"

"I'm at LeRoy Selmons on Cortez Road in Bradenton. I'm sorry, I don't know the address."

"Is it a male or female?"

"Sara, is it a man or a woman? I can't see."

"Oh, my God, it's a kid, it's a little girl," Brea cries.

Sara and Brea stand and hold their hands to their mouth. We watch as Mason does the Heimlich maneuver on a child. She looks like she is about eight years old or a little older.

"Ma'am, is it a man or a woman?"

"I'm sorry. Please hurry, it's a little girl. She looks about eight or ten years old. Please hurry."

We watch in horror as Mason does the Heimlich maneuver on the small girl. Mason places his arms around the standing, conscious girl's torso and makes a fist. In the center of the abdomen, above the belly button and below the ribs, he gives her firm thrusts inward and upward. When nothing happens, he repeats the process. People crowd in and block our view. Brea holds her baby close to her, and Sara and I hold hands. I try to see better, but too many people are standing and blocking my view. Pretty soon people clap and the crowd thins. I can finally see — a woman is hugging her daughter and a man is shaking Mason's hand.

Mason kneels down and speaks to the child and she hugs him. He smoothes her long brown hair and pats the top of her head before he, Donovan, and Vincent join us at our table.

Mason excuses himself to go to the restroom and the ambulance pulls up with lights and sirens on. The parents, still hugging their little girl, walk out with her to meet the ambulance.

Mason joins us and sits down.

"I'm starving. I think I want a steak." He picks up his menu to look it over. Brea, Sara, and I just look at him. He just saved a kid's life and he is looking at a menu.

"Mason?"

He lowers the menu and looks over at Sara.

"You just saved a life," she says, like he doesn't know that.

"Maybe. Maybe she would have coughed it up on her own," he says, raising the menu to look at it again.

"Mason? You just saved a kid's life — don't act like it's not a big deal," Brea says, while rocking her son.

Mason looks over his menu, "What are you guys hungry for?"

"Please excuse me. I don't mean to interrupt."

We all look up.

"I'm Steve Norris, the manager," he says, reaching his hand out for Mason's.

Mason smiles, and shakes Steve's hand. "Hi, Steve, I'm Mason and this is my fiancé, Angel, and our friends, Sara, Donovan, Brea, Vincent, and their son, Arturo."

"I won't be long and I don't mean to interrupt. I just wanted to thank you for jumping in and doing what you did. As you know, if you hadn't stepped in, the outcome may have been much different. As our thanks to you,

LeRoy Selmons would like to buy dinners, drinks, and desserts for you, your beautiful fiancé, and your friends tonight."

"No, really, that isn't necessary. If I hadn't been here, someone else would have stepped in. That is very kind of you, but really, it's not necessary. I'm just thankful it all worked out."

"Thank you and your meals are already taken care of." Steve nods, and looks at everyone before leaving.

"See, Mason, that is a big deal," Sara says.

"I'm just glad that little girl will be going home with her parents tonight."

Mason

Raùl comes in a few days early for Thanksgiving. Angel wanted to cook and have everyone come here, but Mom insisted on having everyone over there, including Josephine and Carl.

"Mason, I need to meet Aunt Rosie at the cottage tonight to try on Momma's wedding dress. Do you want to go or would you like to do something with Vincent and Donovan?"

"I'll go. I need to speak with Raùl about something."

Angel looks over her shoulder, while she brushes her hair.

"About what?"

Think, Mason, think.

"I think I heard Maria's brakes on her car squealing the other day. I need to talk to him about that."

"I didn't notice; you must have good ears." She turns around and puts her long hair up into a high ponytail.

I have good ears or I'm becoming a good liar.

We arrive at the cottage and see a large clothing bag lying across the bed. I look at it, and Angel and Maria both yell at me.

"No, Mason!" Maria shouts. "It's Angel's mother's wedding gown. Don't look. She wants to surprise you with the dress."

"I'm just looking," I say, holding my hands up in surrender.

"No looking; behave or you'll have to leave," Maria says, laughing.

"Come on, Mason, let them be alone to do what they need to do."

I kiss Angel and Maria, then follow Raùl outside. We pass Josephine on the way out.

"I see they ran you both off," Josephine says, laughing as she heads inside the cottage.

"They sure did. Is Carl home?" Raùl asks.

"He's waiting on you both. He suspected this would happen," she says, closing the door behind her.

We walk over and see that Carl is on the front porch with three Bud Lights sitting on a table.

"That took less time than I expected."

"It doesn't take long to make Maria mad." Raúl laughs.

We sit outside talking about the items I asked Raùl to bring with him from Los Angeles.

"I have them hidden in the house, Angel doesn't suspect anything. I was going to hide them from Maria, but that is useless. She knew I was hiding something as soon as I got off the plane."

"Angel will be very pleased with what you are doing." Carl smiles.

"I hope so. I'm a little worried it will upset her. What if she had another idea?"

"Trust me, she will love it." Raùl takes a long drink of his beer. "If it was a bad idea, Maria would have said so."

That is a good point. Angel, Maria, and Josephine walk across the yard, smiling.

I stand and kiss Angel when she reaches me. "That must have gone very well."

"It did; the dress is in much better condition than I thought it would be."

I sit down and Angel sits on my lap.

"Your Uncle Raùl and I will drop it off at the cleaners tomorrow and it'll be good as new."

It's Thanksgiving Day and it's our first Thanksgiving together. Angel and I are going to my parents for dinner. Raùl, Maria, Carl, and Josephine will also be there. We begin our day with Angel cooking a few of her specialty dishes to take over with us.

"You do realize plenty of food will be there?"

"I know, but there is just something about showing up empty handed that doesn't sit well with me."

"They are just glad to have us there. They don't care what we bring as long as we show up."

"I know and I appreciate that. It's just a few dishes, nothing special. I'll just be a few more minutes."

I take a tortilla and scoop up some bean dip onto it.

"Let's leave this dip here, so we can have it for later."

"I made *you* some extra, but *this* is for your parents." She laughs.

I take another scoop and she smacks my hand, laughing.

"Mom said to remind you to bring your notebook with you. She wants to finalize everything for the wedding."

"I have it all ready. Can you believe we'll be getting married next month?"

"It's not soon enough if you ask me. I can't wait to finally have you forever,"

"Mason, whether we get married or not, you already have me forever."

"I know that; I just want to make sure everyone else knows that, too."

I walk over and wrap my arms around her.

"You are so possessive."

"I can't help it." I kiss her and she kisses me back.

We are greeted by my parents and Madison as we pull into my parents' driveway. Raùl and Maria's car is already in the driveway. Josephine and Carl must have rode with them. Dad walks down the stairs and helps me with the food Angel made.

"Angel, this smells delicious," my Dad says holding up a glass dish.

Angel looks back behind her and smiles. "Thank you, it's a bean dip. It was my Momma's favorite recipe. I hope you like it."

"If it tastes like it smells, I'll love it."

We gather around the large dining room table. It is set with a white lace tablecloth and my grandmother's fine china. Mom uses this china only for holidays and special occasions. The candles are lit on the table beside the white lily centerpiece. Dad always buys lilies for my mother.

We snack on appetizers and watch the Macy's Thanksgiving Day Parade while the ham and turkey cook. A family tradition since childhood. After dinner we watch football. Also a childhood tradition.

Carl has the privilege to say the grace today. We stand around the table and hold hands.

"Dear Heavenly Father, We thank you for this wonderful meal before us. We thank you for bringing us all together on such a wonderful occasion. Thank you for keeping us healthy and for all the wonderful blessings we have everyday. We pray that you bless and look after the less fortunate and guide them. In your name we pray, Amen."

We all say "Amen" in unison before taking our seats and enjoying a wonderful meal together.

"So, Angel, we hear your wedding dress is almost ready," Mom says.

"It is, and it's in better condition than I had anticipated."

We mostly talk about the upcoming wedding. Everyone knows where I am taking Angel on our honeymoon but Angel. I want to surprise her and I had to do some research before booking our flights. I needed to get the exact location on the island.

Time to clean up. We guys help — sort of. After dinner and after we all help with cleanup, the guys turn the TV on to watch the football games. I stand at the large bay window and watch the girls outside. Angel has her notebook and pen in hand taking notes. They walk around the yard pointing at certain areas where the bushes and trees are.

"Son, you're missing a great game," my Dad yells from the Lazy Boy recliner.

"I'll be right there."

Angel looks up from the yard and waves to me.

I wave back and smile.

Angel turns her attention back to the activities in the yard. She moves her arms around and Mom nods while Angel writes something else down on her paper. When Angel looks up again and sees that I am still watching her, I decide I need to move. I may be creeping her out, standing at the window, watching her. I sit on the couch and watch the rest of the game.

Once the game is over and the last of the wedding plans are complete, we say our goodbyes. Mom sends home a plate of turkey; she know how much I love left-over turkey sandwiches.

"Buckle up, Beauty."

Angel looks over at me and laughs. She has the seat belt already in her hands. "You like to say that, don't you?"

"I just want you to be safe, that's all."

"You do know that when you're not around, I remember to buckle up on my own."

"I would hope so. I don't want anything to happen to you." I lift her hand and kiss it.

"I had a great time today."

"Good, so did I. I'm glad Carl and Josephine were there. Did you happen to taste her pies?"

"Oh, did she make those?" I had the apple and the crust melted in my mouth."

"I know. Mom said she made all the pies. I wonder if she'll make us one for our wedding."

"Mason, stop it. We are not having pie at the wedding." She laughs.

Later that night, we lie on the couch and watch *Miracle on 34th Street*. It's a family tradition of Angel's and her family. Of course Angel falls asleep in the middle of it. I think that is another family tradition. I don't wake her. We sleep on the couch together until morning.

Angel

I meet with Marilyn and discuss what she would like to see done in her master suite. She already has a beautiful space. I can't imagine why she wants to change anything in here. Sometimes, I think people can have too much money.

We walk through the bedroom and into the two large walk-in closets, the sitting area, and the master bath. Her suite is larger than my old cottage. Once I get an idea of what she would like to have done to her suite, we have tea and crumpets outside on the lanai. She turns the fireplace on and the area warms up quickly. The waterfall is also on and adds to the relaxing ambience. This is definitely a nice space. Very pleased with my work, she tells me how much she enjoys her lanai and how much time she and her husband spend there.

I head home but stop by the jewelry store first. I bought Mason something for Christmas, and I want to see if it's in yet. It's our first Christmas, and I want it to be special. I arrive home and see Mason unloading several large boxes from his car.

"What are you doing?"

"Maria called and said she had some things that belonged to you and asked if I wanted to pick them up."

"I didn't leave anything there." I walk over and help Mason with the last box and follow him into the house. Several other boxes are already on the floor. I open a box and remove the bubble wrap from the small item. Not believing my eyes, I hold the glass snowman Christmas ornament from my childhood.

"Oh, Mason, look." I hold up the fragile ornament for him to see.

He gently takes the glass snowman from my hands and smiles.

"We bought it one year we spent Christmas down here, at one of those shops over on Anna Maria Island."

"It's beautiful."

I anxiously open another ornament and then another. I feel like a kid at Christmas. Mason sits on the floor next to me and helps me. Soon we are sitting among a mess of bubble wrap, old newspapers, and old Christmas ornaments. Mason and I look around and begin to laugh.

"Well, we have a choice," he says. "We can either put them all away or we can put up a tree."

"Really?"

"Really."

"Let's go and get one." I stand up and brush the dust off my clothes.

"I think my grandparents' tree is still here," Mason says, standing and brushing off his clothes. "Go change into something more comfortable, and I'll look in the garage for the tree."

"Yay, I'll make some hot chocolate and play some Christmas music."

"Ok, Beauty, I'll be right back."

"Mason?"

"Beauty?"

"Thank you." I stand on my tiptoes and kiss him. "I love you."

"I love you," he says, kissing me back. "Go and change. I'll be back in a minute."

I put on a pair of black yoga pants and a white tank top and start a pot of homemade hot chocolate. I look through my CDs until I find a Christmas one. Harry Connick, Jr. Who doesn't love Harry? I play it on the surround sound before joining Mason in the living room.

"Need some help?"

"Harry Connick, Jr., huh?" Mason smiles his big dimpled smile.

"It was either that or Bing Crosby's 'White Christmas.'"

"Oh, Harry's good."

"I thought so."

"Hand me the tree stand, will you?"

"Yep."

Once the tree is in the stand and we decide on the perfect spot, I check on the hot chocolate.

"A lot of marshmallows, a little, or more than a lot?" I yell from the kitchen.

Mason walks into the kitchen and stands behind me. "Seven, please."

I look up at him. "Only seven? You do know they are the tiny ones."

"Grandma used to give me and Madison seven when we would stay with her. No more and no less."

"Seven little tiny ones for you and a ¼ of a cup for me."

"Angel?"

"Mason? They are little and I like them." I smile and hand him his mug of hot chocolate.

Mason smiles and takes his mug from me. "We are going to need a dentist for you in the next few months," he says while walking into the living room where the bare tree stands in front of the large bay window.

"This is a perfect spot."

"This is the same place my grandparents put it every year." Mason steps back and looks at the tree fondly.

"It's perfect. Are there any decorations or ornaments that were stored with it?"

"There are still several smaller boxes in the attic. But I thought we could use your ornaments."

"Mason, I thought we could combine the ornaments on the tree to make it ours."

"Well, the tree is definitely big enough for all the ornaments. I'll be back."

When Mason returns, he has three medium-sized boxes with him. We open them and Mason smiles as memories come back to him.

I hold up a small red handprint with Mason's name written across the top. It has a green frayed ribbon weaved through it to use as a hanger.

"Don't say it," Mason laughs.

"Aww, but it's so cute. Look at how little your hands were," I say, holding my hand up to it.

I turn it around and it says in faded words, First grade. Mason and I laugh at the handmade ornaments and at how vintage some of the other ones are.

"These are nice. But I think we need to go out tomorrow and get a few new ones." Mason says, holding up a faded bulb.

"Yeah, I think you're right. Right after church tomorrow?"

"Sounds good. You know, I have never put a tree up in my adult life."

"Never?"

"Not that I can remember."

"Well, Mason, meet your new Christmas tradition. Putting up the Christmas tree, music by Harry Connick, Jr., and homemade hot chocolate with seven tiny marshmallows."

"Here's to our new Christmas tradition: Cheers," he says, holding up his mug of hot chocolate.

"Cheers." I smile as we clink our glass mugs together.

"Color lights or clear lights?" Mason asks, holding up a handful of each.

"Clear," we both say in unison, laughing.

The tree is up and the tiny clear lights are twinkling. Mason and I both opted out of using tinsel on the tree. I am an old-fashioned girl, but I always hated picking that stuff off the tree when I was little.

Mason and I decide it's time for an adult beverage and different music. He returns to the couch with a pen and paper and hands it to me.

"What's this for?"

"It's for your Christmas list."

"Mason, I have everything I need and want right here," I say, handing him the pen and paper back.

"It's up to you, but have you seen those ugly sweaters at K-Mart?"

"Mason, you wouldn't!"

He hands me the pen and paper back with a smile. "Your Christmas list, Beauty."

"Fine."

I tear the paper in half and hand it to him. He smiles and takes it.

"I need a pen." He stands up, walks into the office and returns with another pen. He sits on the other end of the couch and starts to write. He looks over his paper, smiles at me, and writes something else. I wonder what he is writing, I was expecting a small list from him. I think of something else and write it down.

"I think I may need another sheet of paper," Mason says, laughing as he writes some more.

Now I'm beginning to get nervous. "Do you think we should have a spending limit?"

"No, no limit. I want to make sure I get everything on my list. Do you need another sheet of paper?"

"No, I'm good. Do you?" I ask, half afraid of what he's going to say.

Mason writes something else on his list and says, "No, that should take care of everything."

He folds it up until it's in a small square and holds it out for me. When I try to take it, he pulls it back.

"Your list, Beauty," he says, holding his bare hand out for my list.

I fold my list identical to his. I hold both my hands out for him to take my list and for me to take his list at the same time.

"No looking at it until tomorrow," he says, holding his list up.

"No looking until tomorrow," I repeat.

After we exchange our Christmas list, we watch TV and talk a little about the wedding. Mason, Vincent, and Donovan are due to get fitted for their tux's this week. Mason evades any talk of our honeymoon. He just says he is still planning it.

It's Wednesday and Sara, Brea, and I are heading out to do some Christmas shopping at the Brandon Mall. Vincent, Donovan, and Mason are at home having a guys' night in with Arturo. I haven't looked at Mason's Christmas list because I'm almost afraid to.

In Florida, it doesn't really feel like Christmas to anyone originally from Ohio, like Brea and Sara. I am originally from LA, so it feels like Christmas to me. We are wearing sweaters, jeans, and boots, although it's in the 50's. The boots are a girl thing. There is no chance of snow, but boots are a must for any girl in winter.

"I can't believe it's the Christmas season and we are shopping in 50 degree weather," Brea states.

"I know, that's why we moved to Florida. People in Ohio are shoveling snow, already," Sara smiles.

"We should take pictures and post them all over Facebook," Brea laughs.

"Good idea, they'll all hate us."

"Maybe that will be enough to get them down here for a visit."

Christmas music is playing on the surround sound at the mall. Santa and his elves are in the middle of the mall with a large Christmas tree and fireplace set up to make a makeshift workshop. It feels like Christmas time and I love that.

"Come on, we have to get a cup of Christmas," Brea says, excitedly, when she see a Starbucks nearby.

"Cup of Christmas? What's that?"

"Oh, you won't believe it. It's a frozen Chai Tea, and it tastes just like Christmas time," Sara explains.

"I doubt that, but ok."

Sara and Brea wait in line at Starbucks and I reach in my purse to look over Mason's Christmas list. I haven't looked at it yet — I was afraid to. I sit down and slowly open his folded piece of paper.

Angel, Christmas came early for me this year. When I saw you on Vincent's boat that first time, I knew I would never want or need anything else in my life. My life is filled with everything I have ever wanted. Thank you. The only thing that would make it complete is for you to be my wife, and then I will truly have everything. I love you. Mason

Mason

I look at Angel's Christmas list when she is in the bathroom getting ready for bed. I promised I would wait until tomorrow, but I lied. I want to make sure I am able to get everything on her list.

Just as I expected, she didn't list anything worthy of her. (1) Gold hoop earrings, (2) Bruno Mars C.D., (3) Gift card for a mani/pedi, (4) Victoria Secret, Hello Darling body spray (5) A 3-wick candle from Bath and Body Works. I smile and then frown. This is my girl's Christmas list. So simple and plain. She is so much more than plain *or* simple. I refold the list and lay it on my dresser. I hurry into bed and wait for her to join me.

"Does your family do anything special for Christmas?" Angel asks, as she scoots under the covers.

"Mom usually cooks Christmas dinner and we have our gift exchange then. Is there something you want us to do? Have Maria and Raùl over for Christmas?"

"We have a Christmas Eve tradition. We throw a party every year for family and friends. It's mostly appetizers and ham and turkey sandwiches. Do you think it will be all right to have a party this year, here?"

"Angel, this is our home. If you want to throw a party on Christmas Eve, then we will have the biggest party ever."

"Are you sure? I know it's so close to our wedding."

"It's our family and friends. I can't think of a better way to celebrate the birth of Christ than with the people we love the most."

"Good, I'll let everyone know. We are only a little over a week away."

The next few days I get everything on Angel's Christmas list and have the store giftwrap the items. I upgraded a few items on her list and added a few other items. Today, Angel is going Christmas shopping with Sara and Brea. I called Sara up and asked her to shop for Angel tonight. I tell her whatever Angel shows an interest in, to get it and say it's for someone else. I meet Sara after work and give her some money for her shopping spree with Angel.

Angel walks into the house carrying a few bags after her shopping spree with Sara and Brea. I went to Vincent's house to hang out, but decided not to stay long. I wanted to get ready for a night home with Angel. I cleaned the already cleaned house, lit some of her cranberry-scented holiday candles, plugged the Christmas tree in, and turned on the gas fireplace because I know how much she likes its ambience.

When she comes home, I stand up from the couch and set my Scotch down on the coffee table. "Do you need any help with those?"

"No, thank you. I have everything." Angel goes into the spare bedroom and returns empty handed. She makes another quick trip to the car and locks up the house when she re-enters.

"Are you sure you don't need any help?" I ask, still standing.

"Nope, that was the last trip. Would you pour me a glass of a wine while I change?"

"Absolutely, did you have a good time?" I ask, heading into the kitchen to get her a glass of white wine.

"I'll get to that in a minute."

Angel disappears into our bedroom, and I wonder what she is talking about. I pour her a glass of wine and wait for her to return. She made two trips carrying shopping bags. Certainly that is a clear sign of a successful shopping spree. She returns, wearing a pair of gray sweat pants and a white tee shirt. She sits beside me and leans over to kiss me.

"I missed you, too. Did you have a good time?"

"No, I had a great time. But, do you know how hard it is to shop for someone without having any idea of what to get them?"

"I thought we were going to shop for our families together."

"We are, it's you I'm talking about. I went to read your Christmas list and was shocked when there wasn't one."

"You are just now reading my list? I read your list the night we wrote them."

Angel laughs and smacks my arm. "You promised me you would wait to read it until the next day."

"Oh yeah, about that. I lied. I read it that night when you were getting ready for bed. I wanted to make sure I would have time to get everything you wanted."

"I see. Do you lie often?" she smiles.

"We're not talking about me. Why didn't you read my list until now?"

"Well, to be honest. I was scared."

"Scared of what?" I ask, taking a sip of my iced Scotch.

"Of your list. You kept writing and joking about needing more paper. I was scared I wouldn't be able to afford everything you wanted." She sits back into the couch and pulls her quilt over her lap.

"So I take it, you had enough money for everything?" I say, winking at her.

"Mason, that was the sweetest note anyone has written to me. If you weren't so sweet, I would be upset with you," she says, leaning into the crook of my arm.

I kiss the top of her head and inhale her scent. "It's true. There isn't one thing I want or need, except you."

"Do you know how hard it is to shop for someone who has everything?"

"Just put a bow around you on Christmas morning and that is all I want. Pretty easy, I would say."

"Mason, now I have no idea what to get you. I'm running out of time. Our first Christmas together and I wanted it to be special."

"Beauty, with you here, it's already special."

The next few days I do a little more shopping for Angel and pick up the items from Sara that she bought for her from me. Angel sneaks around the house and checks the mail quickly when she sees the mail truck. We shop together for Raùl and Maria; Mom, Dad, and Madison; Carl and Josephine, and our friends. Angel has family in Puerto Rico whom she shops for and sends the gifts over there for them. I know she speaks to her cousins and distant relatives infrequently.

I secretly make phone calls to Raùl and visit the jewelers' store often. I want to make sure our wedding rings are perfect. Angel and I shop for groceries for our Christmas Eve party tonight. Our wedding is one week from tonight and it can't come quick enough.

"Mason, will you help me zip this?" Angel yells from another room.

Angel and I still haven't made love, and I found it was easier for me to start showering and dressing in one of the spare bedrooms. It is becoming quite difficult to keep my composure. I feel like I'm one big walking hard-on. *Please be fully dressed, please be fully dressed*, I silently pray.

"I'm coming," I say, walking into our bedroom while straightening my tie. Angel is standing near the bed, wearing a red form-fitting dress. Her back is to me and she is stepping into a pair of black stilettos. Her long black curly hair is pulled over to one shoulder revealing her bare back.

"Wow" is all I say.

She turns around and smiles at me. "I'm not completely dressed yet. Maybe once you zip it, you won't be saying that."

"Beauty, you are still stunning."

She stands on her tiptoes and kisses me. "Your ability to compliment me is why I love you. Well, that is one of many reasons why I love you."

"And I love you wearing that dress, now turn around." I zip her dress, and it is a perfect fit. She turns around and kisses me again.

"One week from today, we'll be getting married." I smile and I lift her up and kiss her again.

"Mr. and Mrs. Myles," she smiles.

"I wish it was tonight."

"Me, too." I set her down and she straightens my tie. "Do you have a pin for your tie? It keeps moving to the side."

"No, I don't have one. It's because it's a new tie and it's still stiff."

"No tie pins, huh? Hold on." Angel walks over to her dresser and pulls out a small red gift with a white ribbon and bow.

"Here, an early gift."

"Another tradition?"

"I can't help it. I'm an old-fashioned girl." She smiles.

I walk over to my nightstand and pull out a gift wrapped in gold paper with a red bow. Walking over to her, I can't help but smile. I hand her the small gift and say, "You first."

She places the gift she is holding on top of the bed and takes the one I am holding.

"Mason, I already know without looking at it that it is too much."

"Just open it."

Angel carefully removes the wrapper revealing a Jareds jewelry box. She looks up from the box to me. I nod towards the box. She carefully removes the lid and stares at the diamond and gold necklace and matching earrings in the box. I just watch her. She doesn't say anything but gently runs her fingers over them.

"Here, let me," I say, reaching for the jewelry box. She still doesn't say anything but just stares at the necklace. I remove the diamond and gold necklace and hold it out for her to see.

"That is the most beautiful necklace I have ever seen." She looks at me with tears in her eyes.

"Turn around, Beauty."

She does. She always does what I ask. She knows I would never hurt her or put her in harm's way. I fasten the necklace and she automatically touches it. I walk her to the full-length mirror for her to see. Her tears are streaming down her flawless face.

"It's beautiful, you shouldn't have."

"Angel, it doesn't even compare to your beauty," I say, wiping the tears from her cheek. "You're messing up your makeup," I lie.

She laughs and sniffles. "Please give me my present now," I say.

"I almost don't want to give it to you."

I clear my throat and hold my hand out for my gift.

She laughs and walks over to the bed to get it. "All right, but don't laugh."

"Never." I smile and carefully remove the red wrapper. I don't say it, but it has been a while since I have been excited about receiving a Christmas gift. Julia would buy me thoughtless gifts such as an expensive but ugly glow-in-the-dark garden gnome that I donated to Goodwill but told her was stolen. She also once gave me a certificate for a colonic. Christmas was always about me gifting to her. The worst gift she ever gave me was … naw, I don't want to think about it, but when she gave it to me I thought about making her Valentine's Day gift a mop. The second-worst Christmas present she ever got me was a book titled *The Idiot's Guide for Dummies to Teach Them How to Please a Woman in Bed.* Yeah, Julia was the type of girl who would bring as gifts diapers to a virgin's bridal shower or a sex manual to a 100-year-old man's birthday party. Julia liked for me to buy her really expensive perfume, but if she wants to smell really good she should rub onions and garlic behind her ears — only one thing smells better than Italian food, and that is Angel.

I smile up at her and hold up the jewelry box from Jareds Gallery of Jewelry and say, "Great minds think alike," and we both laugh. I focus my attention back to the box and open it carefully. *I have never received jewelry before.* Inside the box is a beautiful gold tie pin. I smile and look at her. She has a smile to match mine. "It's beautiful. I truly love it."

"Really?"

"Really, thank you."

I remove the square tie pin and read the words engraved into it. *Forever and Always.*

I hand it to her and she puts it on me. "There, now it's perfect."

"Angel, thank you." I kiss her and she wraps her arms around my neck. She opens her mouth for me to enter. I lift her up and she wraps her long tan legs around my waist. I moan and walk her to the edge of the bed.

"Oh, God, Mason."

She tries to grind against me and I think I will come undone. I begin to lay her on the bed and the doorbell rings.

I stop mid air and try to get my bearings. *Please go away.* I don't move or say anything. Angel is breathing heavily; I can feel the rapid rise and fall of her chest. When the doorbell stops, I begin to kiss her again and then the doorbell rings again.

I slowly begin to set her on the floor. "Maybe they'll go away," she whispers.

"I wish. Get the door. I need a minute or a cold shower or both." We don't laugh and she reluctantly walks out the bedroom, closing the door behind her. In one more week, I'll finally have her. I'm not sure I can wait that long. I look down and my dick is bulging through my dress pants. *Think about lacerations, EKG's, and skin tears or Julia. Yuk, that'll take care of it.* I hear Carl and Josephine first. Then Mom, Dad, Madison, Maria, and Raùl.

I walk out and greet our guests with my biggest smile. Brea, Sara, Donovan, Vincent, and Arturo arrive last. I help Angel set the food out and put some Christmas music on the surround sound. The doorbell chimes and Brea answers it for us.

"I invited Emma and her son, James. I didn't want them to be alone on Christmas Eve."

"That is a great idea." Angel and I get the drinks out on the bar and the doorbell rings again.

"I also invited Alec," I say, smiling.

"Do you know what this means?"

"Angel, this means nothing. We invited our friends to our home for a Christmas party. That is all it means." She smiles as she looks out into the living room at our guest.

"Angel?"

"Mason, I have to go mingle." She smiles and quickly walks away from me.

Angel

I walk away from Mason before he can tell me not to interfere with Emma and Alec. I'm just going to give a little shove if I need to. I have never met her son before, so I am excited to get to know him. I look over and see a little blond hair boy holding on to her leg for dear life.

I walk over to them. Brea and Sara are already talking with them. I pass Alec on the way.

"Hi, Alec, so glad you could make it. Make yourself at home."

"Here, Angel," he says, handing me a bottle of wine. "Thank you for inviting me. That was very nice of you."

I take the wine from him and hug him. "I'm glad you could make it. I really never had a chance to thank you for everything you did for me when I was in the hospital."

"No thanks needed. I'm just glad it all worked out." He smiles.

"Well, thank you and thank you for the wine. Mason is setting up the bar if you want to head out there. Do you already know Vincent and Donovan?"

"I do; we are racquetball buddies," he says, laughing.

"Oh, yeah, that's right. Let me introduce you to my Aunt and Uncle."

"We already met in the hospital. I'll go find Mason. Do you want me to take this with me?" he asks, pointing at the gifted bottle of wine.

"Yes, thank you."

I look over at Emma, who is kneeling down and talking to her son. I go under the Christmas tree and remove a large wrapped gift with James' name on it. I smile and walk over to where they are standing. They both are still standing near the front doorway.

"I'm so glad you guys made it." I hug her with one arm.

"I don't think we can stay long," she looks down at her leg and the four-year-old holding on to it.

"Let me try something first."

She nods.

I kneel down so I am eye to eye with James. "Hi, James, I'm Angel."

"Hi," he whispers, pushing his head harder against Emma's leg.

I hold the Thomas the Train-wrapped gift out for him.

"Look what I have for you." I shake the gift and he looks over.

"This is for James, that's you." I shake it again and hold it out for him.

He lets go of his Mom's leg and takes the oversized gift from me. It's heavy so I keep ahold of it with him.

"Do you want to open it?"

He nods. I lay the gift on the floor and Emma kneels down with us. James smiles up at his mother. "Look, Momma, a present for me."

Emma smiles and ruffles his blond hair. "I see it, but what do you say?"

"Thank you, Miss Angel."

"You're welcome, buddy."

James excitedly opens the gift and throws the paper on the floor. He smiles the biggest smile I have ever seen on a child.

"Look, Momma, a train. Miss Angel got me a train like Thomas the Train."

I smile and say, "I'm glad you like it. Do you want to put it together and play with it?"

"May I?"

I pick up the rest of the wrapping paper and stand. "You may; let me get someone to help you, ok?"

"Thank you, Miss Angel. You're the best," James says, hugging my leg. I ruffle his blond hair. Buddy, you are more than welcome. I'll be right back." I look over at Emma and ask, "Want a glass of wine?" She nods and starts opening the large train box. "I'll get someone to help with that. Be back in a minute."

"Angel?"

I look back and she mouths, "Thank you."

"It's my pleasure." I walk into the kitchen with a handful of wrapping paper. After placing it in the trash, I ask Alec, Vincent, and Donovan to help put together a train set. They all walk into the family room and gather in a circle of the floor. I watch Emma introduce everyone to James. Arturo begins to cry and I walk over to the tree and remove his gift from under the tree.

I give the small gift to Brea. "Arturo's gift."

"I hope it's a boob full of milk." She laughs.

"Brea, shut up." I laugh. "It's not and if he's hungry feed him."

"Angel, look at my little chunky boy. He has been putting on weight from drinking all that milk — all he wants to do is eat. He likes boobs. Like father, like son."

Brea opens the gift and shakes the rattle for Arturo. "Look what Auntie Angel got for you," she says in that baby voice I rarely hear from her. "Do you like it?"

Arturo coos and I smile.

Brea says, "It's not a boob and yet he still likes it." We both laugh and Arturo coos again.

I walk around and see that everyone is eating appetizers and drinking. The guys are playing with the train set with James, and Vincent is holding Arturo. Arturo startles when the train whistle blows. I walk over to Mason, who is standing near his Dad.

"Do you think I should put some hand sanitizer out because of the baby?"

"No, he's fine."

"I'm worried about all the germs — he's still so small."

"He'll be fine; the germs will actually help build up his immune system. This time next year he'll be crawling around eating bugs and dirt. He needs to build up his immune system now. After the age of six weeks, it's good to start allowing babies to be exposed to some germs. No one is sick, so he should be fine."

I look up at Mason, "Really?"

"I'm afraid so. If Brea and Vincent are lucky, bugs are all he'll eat."

"Um, Mason, we aren't having any boys. Just so you know."

"Angel, girls eat bugs, too."

"Ugh, I better get my kisses in now, while his mouth is still clean." I smile and walk over to the group on the floor playing with James.

"Look, Miss Angel, look how fast it goes."

"Wow, James, that is very fast. I'm so glad you like it."

"Momma said my Daddy loved trains when he was my age. I think he would like this train."

I look at James and he has a sad look on his face.

"Buddy, I think your Daddy wishes he was here to play with you right now," I say.

My eyes fill up with tears and I want to say something but I can't form the words. Emma is hugging her son, and I am amazed at how well they both are adjusting. Emma is 26 and raising a four-year-old son alone.

I walk away and head into our bedroom so I can pull myself together.

Mason follows me in. "What's wrong?" he asks, walking over to comfort me. He wraps me safely in his arms. I can only shake my head and cry.

"It's all right." He kisses the top of my head and leaves his mouth there.

"I love you. I just want you to know that."

Mason leans his head back and says, "I know that and in one week these will be happy tears."

"Don't ever leave me."

"I'm not going anywhere."

"Mason, promise me you'll never leave me or our kids. I don't think I could take it if you left us."

"Angel," he says, cupping both his hands on my face. "I'm not leaving you, ever."

"Ok, I don't think I can do what Emma does everyday: put a happy face on when your heart is broken."

"Angel, she does what she has to do for her son. She is a strong and brave woman."

"She really is."

"Go dry your tears and put on a happy face. We have a party and kids out there depending on you."

"Ok, I'll be out in a few minutes. Will you go play with James for a few minutes?"

"I sure will. See you in a minute."

Once I am done, I walk out and see Mason and Alec playing with James on the floor. Emma, Sara, and Brea are standing near the bar within seeing distance of James. Josephine, Lilly, and Maria walk over to me.

"Angel, this is a lovely party." Josephine smiles.

"Thank you, I am so glad you made it. I hope you're having a nice time."

"We are having a wonderful time."

"Do you want to get the food out on the table now?" Maria asks, looking at the food on the counter.

"I think now would be a good time, thank you." We all carry the food to the table and uncover everything. Lilly places the serving spoons out, and Josephine announces that the food is ready.

Once everyone is standing around the table, Carl asks, "May I say the prayer this evening?"

We gather into a circle and hold hands. I am standing beside Mason when James squeezes in between us. He holds my hand with his small hand. I look down at him and smile before looking over at Mason. I look around the room and everyone is bowing their heads and closing their eyes. James squeezes my hand and I look down at him. He smiles and closes his eyes.

"Dear Heavenly Father, we thank you for bringing us all here together to celebrate the birth of Jesus Christ. We pray that you watch over our family and friends and keep them safe. Thank you for the food in front of us and bless those less fortunate. Please help us all to remember the true meaning of this holiday season. In your name we pray, Amen."

"Amen."

I open my eyes and look around. James squeezes my hand, and I kneel down to get closer to him.

"Miss Angel, did you know that tomorrow is Jesus' birthday?"

"I know, that's why we are all here tonight. To celebrate his birth. We also have a birthday cake for dessert. Do you want to sing 'Happy Birthday' to Jesus after we eat?"

"I am a really good singer. Momma says I sing like an angel," he smiles, proudly.

"James, are you hungry?" his mother asks.

"Coming, Momma. I got to go. Momma don't like us to waste food," he says, darting off to be with Emma.

Mason and I stand at the kitchen island and watch everyone mingle and interact with each other. Sara and Alec seem to be getting along. I'm glad to see that.

"I like this tradition," Mason says, touching my arm slightly.

I look over at him, "You do."

"There is no better way to celebrate a holiday than with our friends and family."

"I agree. This is Aunt Maria's tradition. She and Raùl started it before I was born. We would all get together on Christmas Eve, all the kids would have one present to open and we would eat, listen to Christmas music, and have a birthday cake for baby Jesus. I missed it the last couple of years because of Jim. I didn't realize how much I missed it until now."

"Well, those days are behind you. From here on out, we will carry on this tradition and many more."

I lean into Mason and he wraps his arms around me. "I love you, Beauty."

"I love you, Handsome."

After everyone eats and we sing "Happy Birthday" to Jesus, everyone begins to leave. Brea, Vincent, and Arturo are the first to go. They want to get the baby to bed so Santa Claus can hurry up and come. Mason and I bought all the families a small gift and we hand them out to them as they leave. Emma and James are next to leave. James gives me a big hug and thanks me. Alec helps Emma load up the train set in Emma's small car. Alec says his goodbyes before leaving.

I want to stand at the doorway and watch the interaction between Emma and Alec but Mason stands in front of me and closes the door behind him.

"Give them some privacy." He smiles.

"I was," I lie.

Madison is next to leave.

Mason, Bruce, Donovan, Carl, and Uncle Raùl light the outdoor fireplace and open a new bottle of Scotch. Aunt Maria, Josephine, Lilly, Sara, and I begin to clean up. Once everything is cleaned up and put away, Lilly opens a new bottle of wine and pours everyone a glass. We turn the music up and join the guys outside on the lanai.

"That was quite a party," Bruce says, sitting next to Lilly. "Everything was delicious," he adds.

"Thank you, Bruce. I'm just glad everything turned out," I smile. Mason sits down beside me and intertwines our fingers together.

"This time next week, it'll be a whole different kind of party," Raùl says, refilling his glass.

Mason looks at me and smiles. "I'll finally marry the love of my life," he says, lifting my hand to his lips and kissing them. "I'm glad we decided to move the time up. Midnight on New Year's Eve sounded perfect, but in reality, it's a little late for a wedding."

"True, but 6:30 p.m. is a great time. With the time change and it getting dark earlier, this will be a perfect time for a wedding." Lilly smiles.

"Everything is all finalized. It's all a waiting game now. I just wish I knew where we were going on our honeymoon so I knew what to pack."

Mason has taken this week and the next two weeks off from work. The entire office is closed and the employees are thrilled. He said his staff said they have never been off for the holidays before and they are looking forward to spending the holidays at home with their families. Some of his staff flew to be with their families out of state; some are going on cruises while the others are staying home. Mason has arranged with another doctor to be on call for Mason during his time off, and Mason will return the favor sometime during the summer.

Mason

Everyone leaves, and Angel and I unwrap one gift each. Aunt Maria and Uncle Raùl left two presents under the tree before they left. I hold my gift. The card reads "To Mason. From Santa. Please open on Christmas Eve." I smile, open it, and see a pair of Christmas sleep pants with green elves and a new white tee shirt. Angel's gift card reads "To Angel. From Santa. Please open on Christmas Eve." She opens her gift and sees that it is a new red eyelet nightgown.

"Another tradition?"

"I'm a traditional girl, but I didn't expect this tonight. They surprised me with these. If you don't want to wear those, you don't have to."

"And break tradition, not on your life."

While Angel is in the bathroom getting ready for bed, I place all of her Christmas gifts under the tree. I want them to be already under the tree for her in the morning. Just like if Santa had brought them.

She walks out of the restroom with her makeup removed from her face; her hair is in a high ponytail, and she is wearing her Christmas nightgown. She is stunning to look at. I pull the covers back for her to get in. She crawls over the large bed until she is resting in the crook of my arm. She smells like peaches and cinnamon.

I inhale her and she laughs. "You always do that."

"I know. I used to secretly inhale you, but now I just do it openly. I hope I don't do it in public. That may creep some people out."

"I inhale you, too. It's a very relaxing smell and it always calms me."

"We are just two creepy people in a pod, aren't we?" I laugh.

"Yeah, I guess we are. Good night, Mason."

"Sweet dreams, Beauty."

The next morning I wake up to the smell of coffee. I already know without looking that Angel is up.

I pull on my shirt and walk out into the living room. The tree is lit, the fireplace is on, and Angel is on the couch covered up with her mother's quilt. She is holding her cup of coffee and staring at the tree. I don't think she sees or hears me.

I slowly walk over to her, and she looks up.

"Merry Christmas, Beauty." I sit down next to her and she leans into me and I open my arms for her. "Why the sad face?"

"Merry Christmas, Mason. I'm just thinking of where my life was this time last year and where I am today."

"That's why you look so sad?"

"No, I just wish my Mom and Dad were here to see me, to meet you. They would love you."

I hold her close and rub my hand up and down her thin cold arm to warm it. "I believe they can see us. I also believe they are watching and looking over you."

"I believe that, too. I just miss them."

"I know you do and I am sorry."

"I wish they were here for our wedding. Can you believe that in six days, we'll be married?"

"I can, Mrs. Myles." I also beam. "We'll be married and you'll be all mine forever. It's so close yet feels like it's so far away."

"It's close, I hope we can get everything done."

"Angel, let me get a cup of coffee, then you can open your Christmas gifts. I want to take one day at a time, and today we are celebrating our first Christmas together."

"I'm sorry, I have a lot going on in here." She points to her temples.

I laugh and stand to get myself a cup of coffee. "My girl never rests."

When I return with my coffee, Angel is sitting on the floor near the tree holding a gift. She smiles and she looks like a child on Christmas morning. I sit in front of her on the floor and cross my long legs to mimic hers.

She hands me the small silver gift with a huge grin. "Open it."

I set my coffee down, take the gift, and shake it, and she laughs. Carefully opening the gift, I uncover a beautiful wooden case. I run my fingers across it and feel its smoothness. I carefully open the box and inside is a velvet bag. Inside the bag is a set of beautiful writing pens. There is also a business card that reads *Turning Red Woodturnings by Eric Laudenbacher*. I pick up one of the two pens and run my fingers over it.

"This is beautiful." I look up at Angel and she is smiling. "Is this wood?"

"It is, the pens can be made of exotic or native woods, acrylics, or antler, and everything is turned on a wood lathe. I chose hickory wood for you. I hope you like it."

"Angel, I love this. What a thoughtful gift. How did you find these?"

"When I went to Ohio with Sara and Brea, we went to an art show at the Secrest Auditorium in Zanesville. Eric, who makes these pens, described great detail everything that goes into making these. He was very nice and very informative. He takes great pride in making these so I bought you, your Dad, and my uncle a set. I also bought a set for Carl."

"Thank you very much. We'll need to get the website address so when I use up the ink up we can get more pens."

"They have replacement cartridges so you can reuse them." She smiles.

I open the pen and scribble something on the used wrapping paper. "It writes nice, too." I hold up the paper and Angel laughs. *Angelica Hope Myles.*

I look under the tree and reach for a red wrapped gift and hand it to Angel.

"Your turn." I hand Angel the box and she smiles before she shakes it.

"I just love Christmas."

"I can see that, now open it."

She tears the wrapper off, then she removes the lid to the square jewelry box. She picks up the silver charm bracelet and shakes it. She smiles when it jingles. She lowers it and begins to look at each charm. I watch her as she smiles and fingers each charm.

"Mason?"

"Beauty?"

"This is from our first year together, isn't it?" she asks while touching the sailboat charm.

"It is."

"Is this a Pandora Bracelet?"

"No it's different. It's handmade from a woman and the charms were handmade just for you. Her business is called Noodle Noo and her name is Missy MacKenzie Swain." Missy is a friend of mine and her business, Noodle Noo, is the nickname her parents gave her when she was a little girl. Even today, they still use it.

"You told her what to add to this and she did? This is so beautiful. She does great work."

"I think so, too. She was very easy to work with."

She smiles and carefully looks at each charm: a high-heel shoe with a bow on the back, a wine glass, a bottle of Scotch, a few book charms of her favorite books, a sailboat, a dolphin, and an engagement ring.

"I thought you could add more charms or books to it, if you wanted."

She looks up at me. "I love it, thank you." She holds her tiny wrist out for me, "Would you mind?"

I take the bracelet and fasten it to her wrist.

She smiles and shakes her wrist. "I love this sound."

"There's a spinoff from that gift. Do you want it now?" I hand her another gift and she smiles.

She opens the box and reveals small picture frame charms. She picks up the first charm and it is a picture of her mother. She holds it to her heart and begins to cry. "Oh, Mason," she says before lunging into my arms.

"Don't cry, Beauty," I say, stroking her long hair.

"I love you — you are the most thoughtful man in the world."

"I love you, too. Look at the rest of them, there's more."

Angel sits down and empties the box of charms out on her lap. The charms include a picture of her Aunt Rosie, her father, grandparents, and a cousin who died very young. I also included my grandparents' photos with them.

"I don't understand. If these are charms, why aren't they on my bracelet?" she asks wiping her teary eyes."

"These are charms of our deceased loved ones. I thought, if you wanted, you could add them to your wedding flowers or include them on the ring bearer's pillow, or something like that." I lift her chin with my fingers. "Knowing you like I do, I thought you would want to include them in our wedding."

"That is a great idea, I never thought of that."

"I can't take all the credit; Missy MacKenzie Swain came up with the idea. I just had to come up with the pictures."

"I think I love her." Angel laughs and sniffles.

I cough and clear my throat.

"Oh, I love you, more." She laughs and sniffles again.

"I would hope so."

We open the rest of our gifts and get ready to go to Maria and Raùl's for Christmas dinner. Carl and Josephine will also be there. We have dinner and exchange gifts before heading to my parents' house for yet another dinner and another gift exchange.

"Mason, I think you should tell me where we are going on our honeymoon."

"You do, huh?"

"I do. It's my honeymoon too and I need to know what to pack. I appreciate the surprise, but I want to make sure I have the right clothing and things."

"Angel, for our honeymoon, I made reservations at the Ritz Carlton in Sarasota for a week and then we are flying to Puerto Rico for another week to spend some time with your extended family."

"Oh, Mason, have you talked to my family?"

"I did with the help of Raùl and Maria. Their accent is pretty heavy and as you know, I don't speak Spanish."

I throw my arm around him and kiss him.

"They are pretty excited to see you again."

"It has been years since I have seen them. Thank you so much."

The week flies by, I am responsible for picking up the tuxes and wedding rings, and Angel is responsible for picking up her wedding dress and flowers. I meet with Raùl and we go over some wedding plans with Maria. I get only one chance and I want to make sure I get this right.

Later that night, Angel and I are going over some last-minute wedding details.

"Angel, do we have a wedding song?"

"Oh, no. We don't have a song."

"We need one, right? Something to dance to."

"We don't have a song. Have we ever danced to a slow song?"

I pour her a glass of diet Pepsi. Our wedding is in two days, and she has lived on celery, carrots, and diet soda. "We danced to some at Brea and Vincent's wedding."

"Oh, what about 'A Thousand Years' by Christina Perri?"

"I love that song. I think it's perfect."

"Yay, we have a song," she says, sitting on my lap.

She adds, "This time tomorrow, I'll be staying at my Aunt and Uncle's house."

"I was wanting to talk to you about that. What if you stay here and I promise I won't look at you?"

"No, I don't believe you. No seeing the bride before the wedding."

"I don't want to be apart from you," I say, wrapping my arms around her waist.

"Me, either, we haven't been apart in months. I'm going to miss you."

"Me, too, it's going to be a long two days."

"Just look at the end result," she smiles.

I look up at her. "You'll be mine, forever."

"There'll be no getting rid of me."

"Promise?"

"Promise."

After the rehearsal dinner the following day, I drive Angel home to her Aunt and Uncle's cottage. Supposedly, the groom seeing the bride on her wedding day is bad luck. Maybe people worry about the honeymoon getting started early. I put the car in park and get out to open Angel's door. I reach my hand in and she takes it. She stands tall and confident.

"You know, I like all of your traditions except this one."

"Me, too. This is harder than I thought."

We start to walk towards the front door. "You know, we haven't slept apart in a long time. I hate returning to the beach house without you."

"I hate staying here without you. But tomorrow night, we'll be Mr. and Mrs. Mason Myles."

I smile and Angel leans into me and I wrap my arms securely around her. "Husband and wife forever."

"I can't wait — you are my dream come true, Mason. I can't believe we are counting down the hours."

"I know I need to let you go, but I don't want to." I kiss her on the tip of her nose.

"It's almost midnight."

"Are you going to turn into a pumpkin?" I tease.

"No, but we will have years and years of bad luck."

"I doubt that." I kiss her goodnight. "Get in there and I'll get your things from the car."

"I love you, and I'll see you at the altar tomorrow."

"I love you, more, and tomorrow can't come fast enough. Get in there before I change my mind. Sweet dreams, Beauty."

"Goodnight, Mason," she says, walking into the house and closing the door behind her.

I go to the car and remove her overnight bag, her makeup case, and a garment bag. When I walk into the house, the clock on the wall reads 12:01.

"Is Cinderella hiding?" I laugh while placing everything on the dining room table.

"Yes, Mason, she is," Maria says, smiling.

"I thought she would be."

"I can hear you," Angel yells from the other side of the bedroom door.

I smile and walk over to the bedroom door. "Angel?"

"Yeah," she whispers.

"I'm leaving; call me if you need me or if you want to talk."

Angel cracks the door slightly and reaches her hand out for me. I take it and lift it to my mouth to kiss it. Leaning my head into the door, I whisper, "I love you so much."

"I love you, too," she says, sniffling.

"Don't cry, Beauty, not today."

She laughs and sniffles. "They're happy tears, but I'm going to miss you."

"Me, too. I'll be at Mom's tomorrow, supervising the setup. Call me when you are on your way, and I'll make sure I'm hidden."

"Ok, I love you."

"I love you, more."

"Don't forget my luggage and the garment bags for the honeymoon."

"I won't."

"Goodnight, Mason," she whispers.

"Sweet dreams, Beauty." I lift her hand and kiss it again. I run my lip across her knuckles and kiss her again. I reluctantly let go and she retracts her hand inside the bedroom and closes the door softly. I stay there with my head resting against the door. I am waiting for I don't know what.

"Mason, it's for only one night," Maria says softly.

I turn around and I realize how pathetic I look. I stand tall and square my shoulders. "She is a hard woman to stay away from."

"We think so, too."

"Keep her safe until tomorrow, will you?"

"Mason, she'll be fine. We won't even leave the house."

"Thank you," I say, walking over to hug her. "Have a good night and thank you, again."

"Good night, and we'll see you tomorrow at your parents' house."

"Yes, you will. I am marrying the woman of my dreams in a few hours. Call me if you need anything."

"Mason, go so I can come out already." Angel laughs from the other side of the bedroom door.

"I love you, too, and I'm going," I tell Maria. "She's so bossy and we aren't even married yet." I laugh.

"I can hear you."

"Ok, ok, I'm leaving." I leave, smiling. *God, I love that girl.*

I drive home and walk into a too-large empty home. I decide to have a nightcap before bed. I go into my closet and pull on a hoodie. I inhale — the hoodie smells like Angel. I inhale again. *Man, I really do have a problem.* I soon realize this is the hoodie Angel usually wears. After I pour myself a nightcap, I open the lanai door and smile.

"What are you two doing here?" I ask Vincent and Donovan, who are sitting at the outdoor table playing cards.

"What took you so long?" Donovan asks, slamming his cards down and then yelling, "Blackjack!"

"Sorry, I didn't realize I was hosting a party tonight."

"Sara and Brea are with Angel, and Arturo is spending the night with his grandparents. So, this is your bachelor party. As per your request, no strippers. Get some chips and we'll have what you're having." Donovan nods to my glass of Scotch.

"This is nice; my two best men are throwing me a bachelor party."

Raùl and Carl come walking up from the beach. "Don't start the party without us," Carl laughs.

"This is a nice surprise."

"Well, Angel is having a slumber party, compliments of Sara and Brea, so we came over here to get away from all that giddiness," Raùl says as he takes a seat at the round outside table. "Texas Hold 'em?"

"Now you're talking," Vincent says, shuffling the cards.

"Cigars?" Donovan, asks.

"Got 'em, Cuban at that," Raùl smiles.

"My man," Vincent smiles.

I walk back into the house and put some pretzels in a bowl and open a can of mixed nuts. I grab two bottles of Scotch and some glasses before heading back outside. I make two trips outside before I take my seat at the table.

At 3:00 a.m. I finally call it a night and stumble to bed. I text Angel and realize just how drunk I am.

M: I love you and in 15 hours, you'll be all mine.

I wake up to the smell of coffee, talking from the other room and my phone alerting me about a text massage. I check my phone first in hopes it's Angel.

A: Good morning, Handsome. Thank you for my beautiful flowers. I hope you slept well on my side of the bed. I love you and I miss you terribly.

I look down and she is right, I am on her side of the bed. I scoot over to my own side as if she is watching me.

M: Good morning to you, too, soon-to-be Mrs. Myles, and you are welcome. I slept quite well for being drunk and no, I am not on your side of the bed.

A: Mmm, you are becoming quite the liar. I love and miss you. Don't mess up the seating chart for the wedding. I left detailed instructions on where I want everything. I love you. [Symbol]

M: Don't worry, I have it under control. Enjoy your day. I love you, more.

I shower and dress quickly. It's 11:00 and I should have been up by now. When I walk out into the living room, I am surprised to see everyone is still here. I am more surprised to see everything is cleaned up and in its place.

"We were instructed to stay here and make sure you don't forget anything — like showing up for the wedding. Angel can be very intimidating," Raùl laughs.

"Who you telling," I say, walking over to get a cup of coffee. Once we finish off the pot of coffee, I head over to my parents' house. When I arrive, I am surprised to see the entire yard is being transformed into a fantasy land. The landscapers are bringing in trees, planters, and flowers. The yard is manicured to perfection. They are stringing clear lights in all the trees and bushes. The chairs are all covered in gold chair covers with large bows on the back. It dawns on me that today, I am marrying the girl of my dreams. I run my hands through my hair and sit down.

Mom walks over to me and bends down to kiss me. "How are you?"

"Up until a minute ago, I was fine. It's really happening, isn't it? In a few hours I am going to marry the girl of my dreams. She's the best thing that has ever happened to me. What if I screw it up? What if I can't be what she deserves?"

Mom sits down beside me and takes my hand. "Mason, you and your sister are my pride and joy. I loved you before I was even pregnant for you. Your father and I gave you a good foundation: We let you succeed, and we let you fail. We guarded you but let you grow. You worked hard to be where you are today. Marrying is a life lesson. Mason, you and Angel will fight and argue, you two will disagree. But in the end none of that will matter. You love her and I have never seen you happier. Be honest with her and never forget, she is your best friend. Mason, you have all the qualities that a man needs to be a good husband and father. I have no worries that you will be anything but wonderful."

"Mom, a few months ago I thought she might die. Here I am going to marry her. I just want to protect her and keep her safe."

"Mason, you are already a wonderful husband. You have nothing to worry about. Listen to your heart and you will never go wrong."

"You make it sound so easy."

"I have never lied to you. Your heart will always lead you in the right direction. Just listen to it."

"I hope I can live up to your expectations."

"Mason, you already have." Mom pats my hand.

"Mason, Angel's pulling in." Dad yells from the side of the yard.

"She'll kill me if I see her." We both stand and I laugh.

"Well, you better run."

Angel

"Wow, Angel, your mother's dress looks amazing on you." Maria wipes the tears from her eyes. I stare at myself in the mirror and imagine my Momma wearing this dress on her wedding day. I suck in my belly and turn side to side. I stare at the mirror then turn around. I look at the small train in the back of the dress I had added. I didn't want to make drastic changes to her dress, but I did need to update it a bit.

Lilly carries over the veil and places it gently on my head. She steps back and looks at me. "Oh, Angel, you look stunning." She cries and wipes the tears from her cheek.

"Ten more minutes, girls," a voice calls from the hallway.

"That's our cue. Angel, I love you like a daughter and I am so happy to have you in our family."

"Thank you, Lilly. I appreciate that and I love you, too."

Lilly hugs me and walks out of the room.

"It's show time, Pumpkin," Uncle Raùl says, walking into the room.

He stops in his tracks and smiles at me. I can see him swallowing. His eyes well up with tears and I am afraid he is going to cry.

"Angel, I need to go. You look so beautiful; your mother would be proud." Aunt Maria walks over and hands me my bouquet of white daisies.

"Thank you. I love you so much." I hug Aunt Maria and will the tears not to fall. I play with the small picture charms that have been placed on the ribbon of the bouquet. Aunt Maria looks back at me and walks out the door to meet the usher waiting to take her to her assigned seat.

"Here, Angel." Sara dabs my eyes for me. "Don't you dare ruin your makeup."

Brea and Sara hug me. "We'll give you two a minute. Raùl, if she messes up her makeup, I'm blaming you," Brea says, laughing.

"Ok, I'll do my best not to get her crying."

Sara and Brea leave and someone yells, "Five more minutes," from the hallway.

Uncle Raùl slowly walks over to me. "Angel, you look just like your mother in that dress. I almost forgot how beautiful Ana was. I know she is smiling down on you and her heart is filled with joy for you today."

"Oh, Uncle Raùl, I hope so. I miss her so much."

"I know you do, Pumpkin."

"I wish she was here and that she could meet Mason. I love him so much." I begin to cry.

"No, no tears today, Angel. Why the sad tears?"

"Uncle Raùl, what if he realizes that I'm not good enough for him? He has power and wealth, and I have nothing. I have brought nothing into this relationship. But I love him more than I have ever loved anyone."

"Angel, Mason loves you. He does not care about your money or the lack of it. He loves what's in your heart and the way you love with everything in you. He loves the fighter and the beautiful woman you are. Lilly just had the same talk with him about the same thing. Angel, he's afraid he isn't good enough for you."

"He does?"

"He does, Pumpkin."

"It's show time," the wedding coordinator yells from the hallway.

"She really is a bit irritating." I laugh.

"You hired her and she is doing her job. Are you ready, Pumpkin?"

"It's now or never."

"Come on, Angel, Mason is waiting,"

We walk down the stairs and wait in the back of the line. I stay hidden from view of everyone outside. The house is kept dark and it's a little difficult to see. James, who is our ring bearer, looks back at me and gives me a thumb's up. I wave and give him my proudest smile. Madison, Brea, and then Sara walk out. Uncle Raùl and I step up closer to the open lanai doorway. We wait for our cue. The music changes and I can hear shuffling. We get our cue to go and the butterflies come back in my belly full force. I stop and hold my stomach. I take a few cleansing breaths and close my eyes. *I can do this.*

I walk with Uncle Raùl out onto the lanei, down the steps and onto the red carpet. Our flower girl, Mercedes, Mason's cousin, goes first. She is supposed to drop daisy petals along the way to the altar. I hear laughter and I am not sure what that is for. I see all the daisy petals are in one spot. I smile. She must have just dumped them. I keep my eyes down; I'm afraid if I look up I'll see Mason and then I'll start crying.

"Pumpkin?"

I know, I know. I look up and Mason is smiling his big dimpled smile. I immediately relax and smile back. I have missed him. This is the day I have waited for. Uncle Raùl squeezes my arm and nudges me forward. I look at my uncle to let him know I am fine. I look back at Mason; he is dressed in a black tux, a crisp white shirt with a gold tie, and a cummerbund. He is also wearing a white daisy in his lapel. I smile. The wedding song is "A Thousand Years" by Christina Perri. I love this song. The white lights are twinkling, and the candles are all glowing. The entire yard is transformed into a fairytale. When we reach Mason, he steps down from the platform and takes my hand.

I kiss my Uncle, and he takes his seat next to my Aunt.

"You look beautiful," Mason says, walking me up to the platform to stand in front of the preacher. I am too scared to speak, so I look up at Mason and he winks at me. I lean into him and I hear laughter. We listen to the preacher and Mason squeezes my hand to let me know he is here.

Mason and I agreed to make our own vows. I spent last night writing mine from my heart.

I turn at the instructions of the preacher and Mason does the same. I smile at him and clear my throat.

"It's just you and me, Beauty," Mason whispers and takes both my hands in his. I nod.

"Mason, I love you. When I was a little girl, I read books about you. You were the hero, the Prince Charming, the knight in shining armor, in all my books. I thought you were made up: make believe. I thought you were only in the fairytales that I read." I squeeze his hands and a tear falls onto my cheek. "Then I met you and I could not believe you were real. The more time I spent with you, the more I knew you were too good to be true. I have often asked God what I could have done to deserve you. You are kind, loving, sincere, and always a gentleman. You saved me and showed me what it's like to be loved. You never judged me and you showed more patience than I deserved. You are my heart and my life." I sniffle and more tears fall. "You make me want to be a better person. I promise you, I will love you with all that I am and I will try my best to be a person you can be proud of. Mason, I love you more than you can imagine."

Mason leans in and wipes the tears from my cheeks before he kisses me. "I love you, more."

Mason clears his throat, "Beauty, when I first met you I knew you were like no other woman in the world. I knew I had to get to know you and I was right. You are truly like no other. I love you and I want to be with you, forever." Mason smiles and doesn't look away. "You make me want to be a better person, and you make me want to see the world through your innocent eyes. You make me want to protect you, care for you, and love you with everything that I am as a man."

I lean in and kiss Mason. He smiles and kisses me back.

"Angel, we still have the rings to exchange," Mason whispers. The preacher laughs.

"Yes, I'm sorry." I straighten my dress and Mason smiles. James walks up and stands between Mason and me. The preacher says a prayer and blesses our rings.

"Angel, please remove Mason's rings from the pillow."

I nod and bend down to see four rings tied to the pillow that James is holding. I smile at James and stare at the rings. I blink a few times and my heart begins to race. I lean up and look at Mason. I can't see him through the tears. Sara hands me a tissue and I try to wipe the tears enough to see Mason.

"Mason, I don't know what ring to take; there are too many of them on the pillow."

Mason takes the pillow from James and holds it up to me. "Angel, I have two different rings for each of us. It's totally up to you which ones we use. These ones belonged to your parents. With Raùl and Maria's approval, I had them cleaned and the diamonds tightened. These other ones are the ones I bought; if you would rather not use your parents' rings, we can use these. It's up to you, but I wanted you to have a choice." He smiles and wipes away my tears.

"Really, you did that?"

"It's your choice."

I look at the rings and untie my father's ring from the pillow for Mason. Mason smiles and hands the pillow back to James. I say a few words and slip the ring on Mason's finger. To my surprise, it is a perfect fit. I look up and Mason nods at me. He puts my mother's ring on my finger, and it is also a perfect fit.

"Now you may kiss your bride."

Everyone laughs as Mason swoops me up in his arms and I wrap my arms around his neck. We kiss like we are the only two people in the room.

We turn around and smile. The preacher announces, "I would like to introduce you to Dr. and Mrs. Mason Alexander Myles."

I smile and look over at Mason. "Mason, I love you."

"Angel, I will always love you, more."

The End

NOTE

Destined to Love is Book 3 of the *Starting Over* trilogy:

Book 1: *A New Beginning*

Book 2: *Saving Angel*

Book 3: *Destined to Love*

You can follow Mason and Angel and the other characters in *Shattered Dreams:* a spinoff of the *Starting Over Trilogy*, featuring Emma, James, and Dr. Alec Collins.

ACKNOWLEDGEMENTS

Writing has always come easy for me. When I finally put pen to paper, or fingers to keyboard, I had no idea the direction my books would take me, or the roller coaster ride I would be on. My characters figuratively spoke to me day and night. I was shocked by the direction these books traveled. I hope you love Mason and Angel as much as I do.

My husband Rex: Thank you for all you do for me and our family. You have truly been a blessing every day. I don't know where I would be without you. I love you, more.

Carey, John, Derek, Nikki, Chastidy, Rex, Brittany, Amanda, and Katie: Thank you for keeping me grounded and being who you are. Thank you for reminding me what is important every single day. I love you.

Desmond, Samantha, Autumn, Evan, Derek, Dayquan, Darius, Draden, Alyssa, Hailey, Lucca, Tanner, Giovanni, Cain, Lelila, Kylie, DeVonte', Adrienne, Amaya, Dominic, Damien, Caden, and Gemma: Thank you for reminding me that I am somebody; I am your grandma and nothing else matters. I love you all.

My sisters, Martha, Rosa, and Carla: Thank you for loving Mason and Angel as much as I did. Thank you for listening to me go on and on. I love you.

My brothers, George and Frank: Thank you for believing in me. I love you.

My other brother, David: Thank you for believing in me and making these books even better. Thank you for your dedication and hard work. I truly appreciate everything you do. I love you.

Dave Grether, my Business Manager and co-worker: I sold more books than I gave away. All because of you. Thank you.

Thank you, Julie Veitas, Kelly Lanford, Cathy Stotts, Lorraine McDonald, Natalie Neck, Rose Grether, Nichole Taggart, Brittany Kennedy, and Rosa Jones for *always* having my back, pimping my books, helping me at book signings or assisting with the proofreading and editing. I love and appreciate you, more than you know.

All my family, friends, internet friends, and the Manatee County Jail nursing and corrections staff: Thank you all for your support and ideas. I hope I didn't disappoint you.

My close family and very close friends: You may recognize many names and places in *Destined to Love*. I had so much fun incorporating family names and some of my favorite places into this book. You all have definitely helped inspire many of the characters in this book.

To my supporters, readers, and fans. Thank you a million times over. I truly love and read every single review, comment, and piece of advice you leave. I love hearing from you and interacting with you. Your comments and feedback make my day.

Eric Laudenbacher, thank you for allowing me to mention your handcrafted and unique artwork in my book as Angel's Christmas pen set to Mason. I love your handcrafted, wooden pens. To see more of Eric's work, you can go online to Turning Red Wood Turnings by Eric Laudenbacher, or contact him via Facebook.

Missy MacKenzie Swain, owner of Noodle Noo Jewelry/Watches, thank you for allowing me to mention your unique and handcrafted artwork as Mason's Christmas gift to Angel. I love your framed charms. To see more of Missy's designs go to Noodle Noo via Facebook.

Thank you to Cakes and Cups Bakery for making Arturo's mini birthday cupcakes for the Tampa Mashup Book Signing.

I support Indie Authors. If you read this book, please take the time to go on the purchasing site and give it a review. Independent authors count on your reviews to get the word out about our books. Thank you for taking the time to read our books and taking the extra time to review them. We all appreciate it very much.

Disclaimer: People and places in this book have been used fictitiously and without malice.

About the Author: First and foremost I am a wife, mother and grandmother.

I am also a nurse and a new author.

I moved to sunny Florida in 2006 and never looked back. I love fresh squeezed lemonade, crushed ice, teacups, wineglasses, non-franchise restaurants, ice cream cones, boating, picnics, cookouts, throwing parties, lace, white wine, mojitos, strawberry margaritas, white linen tablecloths, fresh flowers and Pinterest. I also love to read and write and to spend time with my family.

My books, thus far, have been inspired by the things I love and the people who influence me, every single day to be a better person.

You may follow me on:

https://www.facebook.com/pages/Brenda-Kennedy-Author

https://twitter.com/BrendaKennedy_

Brendakennedy48@gmail.com

https://www.goodreads.com/author/dashboard